The MAGICAL LAND of BIRTHDAYS

THE MYSTERY OF THE BIRTHDAY BASHER

FROM THE CREATOR OF FLOUR SHOP

by

AMIRAH KASSEM

AMULET BOOKS

NEW YORK

Cataloging-in-Publication Data has been applied for and may be obtained from the Library of Congress.

ISBN 978-1-4197-4028-2

Printed and bound in U.S.A.
10 9 8 7 6 5 4 3 2 1

Amulet Books are available at special discounts when purchased in quantity for premiums and promotions as well as fundraising or educational use. Special editions can also be created to specification. For details, contact specialsales@ abramsbooks.com or the address below.

Amulet Books® is a registered trademark of Harry N. Abrams, Inc.

ABRAMS The Art of Books
195 Broadway, New York, NY 10007
abramsbooks.com

To everyone with a half-birthday!

Together we have the power to make the world a happier place!

Anything is possible if you follow your heart and keep believing.

Sprinkles ✧ ✦ and Smiles

A M I R A H   K A S S E M

CHAPTER ONE

"**AMIRAH!** Phone call!"

Mama's voice carried through the open window, all the way to the backyard, where Amirah was watering a small patch of purple violets.

Amirah jumped up and dropped the watering can, which tumbled onto its side and spilled water all over her bare feet. Amirah didn't mind, though. Now that summer was here, the weather was hot, hot, *hot!* The cool water felt wonderful as it cascaded over her toes.

Amirah dried off her feet at the back door and walked inside. Mama was holding out the phone.

"Who is it?" Amirah asked. But Mama just smiled mysteriously as she gave Amirah the phone.

"Hello?" Amirah said into the phone.

"Hey, it's me," her friend Paulina replied.

"Paulina! What's going on?" Amirah exclaimed. She wandered into the next room and flopped onto the love seat.

"That's, uh, that's actually what I called to ask you," Paulina said.

Amirah tilted her head. There was something odd in Paulina's voice. She usually sounded so cheerful; her sunny laugh was one of Amirah's favorite things about her. But today, there was no sunshine in Paulina's voice. Just sadness.

"Oh, you know, not much," Amirah said. "I planted some violets in the backyard. I want to make candied violets! It's not that hard, but you need super-extra-fresh flowers, and then you dip them in a . . ."

Amirah's voice trailed off when she realized that she was the only one doing any talking. She took a breath. "Hey," she said, trying to start over. "What's wrong?"

There was a long silence. Amirah started to fidget, not sure what she should say next.

At last, Paulina spoke. "I was just wondering why you didn't come to my birthday party," she said, the words tumbling out in a rush. "I thought—I really thought—you'd be there."

Amirah sat up straight, her heart pounding. "You had a birthday party?" she asked. Of course, Amirah knew that it was about time for Paulina's birthday—she kept a list of the birthdays of everybody she'd ever met—but this was the first she was hearing about a birthday party.

"It was yesterday," Paulina said in a small voice. "I mailed the invitations a month ago."

"A month ago?" Amirah repeated, racking her brain as she tried to remember if she'd received an invitation to Paulina's birthday party. No. She hadn't. That was something Amirah would *never* forget. "But—I—I never got one!"

"You didn't?" Paulina said in surprise. "I know I sent one. Yours was the first one I made! You're the birthday princess of Chihuahua after all."

Amirah tried to smile, but her mouth couldn't quite manage it. "I'm so sorry, Paulina," she said. "I would *never* have missed your birthday party if I'd known about it."

"The invitation must've gotten lost in the mail," Paulina mused. "You know, looking back, it did seem a little weird that you didn't RSVP. But I figured you'd just show up anyway."

"I *always* RSVP for a birthday party," Amirah said firmly.

"Don't I know it!" Paulina said with a laugh. Now that she knew Amirah hadn't skipped her party on purpose, the sunshine had returned to Paulina's voice. But Amirah was feeling worse and worse about what had happened.

"I'm so, so sorry," she told Paulina. "I promise I'll find a way to make it up to you."

"Don't worry about it," Paulina said. "These things happen. Besides, I'll have another party next year—and I know you'll be there!"

"You can count on it," Amirah promised.

After Amirah hung up the phone, Mama came into the living room. She could tell right away that something was bothering Amirah. "What's going on?" she asked.

"Oh, Mama," Amirah said. "Paulina had a birthday party yesterday and I didn't show up because I never got the invitation and I know it's not my fault but I feel terrible about it!"

Mama wrapped her arm around Amirah's shoulders. "You didn't get the invitation?" she asked. "That's so odd. The same thing happened to your brother last month."

Amirah's shoulders straightened. "Really?" she asked. "Amir was invited to a birthday party, but his invitation never came?"

Mama nodded. "Yes, it happened during the week you were at camp," she explained. "He was really disappointed to miss his friend's birthday party too."

"It's not just missing the party," Amirah tried to explain. "It's—I feel like I let Paulina down. Birthdays are really important! They deserve to be celebrated by everybody—especially your closest friends! But I didn't even show up for her party. Like I didn't even care."

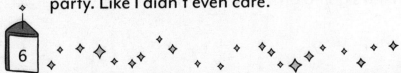

Just saying the words out loud made Amirah feel even worse.

"But you do care," Mama reminded her. "I'm sure Paulina knows that. You know, Amir made a birthday card for his friend and we made a special delivery—"

"Oh, I'm already on it," Amirah assured Mama. She may not have known exactly what to say to Paulina on the phone, but Amirah had plenty of ideas for how to make it up to her.

"Why am I not surprised?" Mama asked with that special smile she saved just for Amirah. She kissed Amirah on the forehead and added, "Just let me know how I can help."

"I will," Amirah replied. "Thanks, Mama."

Amirah practically skipped over to her desk in the corner, where she kept all her favorite art supplies: a thick sketchbook, colored pencils in every color, and—of course—a rainbow-hued assortment of sparkly glitter. Before she got started, Amirah reached into her pocket for the vial of sprinkles she carried everywhere. Amirah was a firm believer in the power of sprinkles to make everything better, from a cupcake to a disappointing day. And she knew better than anyone exactly how powerful sprinkles could be.

Just six months ago, Amirah had embarked on the adventure of a lifetime when she found herself transported to a wondrous world called the Magical Land of Birthdays. There, she had explored enchanted places, solved mysterious puzzles, and even befriended a unicorn! Best of all, Amirah had met her very own B-Buds—birthday buddies who all shared the same birthday. Ever since that magical adventure, Amirah knew deep in her heart that birthdays were more special—and more important—than ever. Just as surely as she knew that someday, somehow, she'd see her B-Buds again. It was hard to imagine waiting until their next shared birthday on January 8, but at least the wait was almost half over.

That's why Amirah would've never skipped Paulina's party—*never*. And that's also why she was so determined to make things right.

Deep in thought, Amirah picked up a pink pencil and started to sketch. Paulina's favorite color was pink, just like Amirah's, and her doll collection was practically a legend in their town. *If only I could bake a cake that looked like a doll*, Amirah thought to herself. But not just any doll. A sophisticated, elegant doll. A doll wearing a gorgeous ball gown—in sparkly pink, of course.

And that's what inspired Amirah to try baking a doll cake for Paulina! She sketched quickly, even though it was hard for her hand to keep up with all the new thoughts popping into her mind.

When she finished sketching, Amirah sat back, studied her cake drawing, and smiled to herself. Yes. It was perfect—perfect for Paulina! Now all Amirah needed to do was get some special ingredients at the store. Mama and Amirah loved to bake more than just about anything else, so they kept their kitchen stocked with all the staples—butter, sugar, flour, eggs. But Paulina's cake would need a little something extra.

Amirah bounded out of the room and found her mother in the kitchen, putting away the clean dishes. "Mama! Can you take me to the store?" she asked breathlessly.

"What do you need?" Mama asked, raising an eyebrow. "We just refilled the sprinkles last week . . ."

"I know," Amirah said with a grin. She showed Mama her sketch. "What do you think? I want to make this cake for Paulina."

"It's beautiful, princess," Mama replied. "She's going to love it."

"I want to get some pink glitter candles . . . and some sugar pearls for the dress. Oh! Maybe I can even get some candy flowers too!" Amirah exclaimed, adding a few more notes to her sketch.

Mama reached for her keys. "I'll get Amir and meet you at the car."

"Thanks, Mama!" Amirah said. She impulsively stood on her tiptoes to give Mama a kiss on the cheek, then bounded out the front door so joyfully that her curls bounced. Despite the heat of the summer day, there was plenty of activity in Amirah's neighborhood. The postal carrier was humming as he traveled from door to door, placing mail in the mailboxes. Amirah's special friend in the neighborhood, Mrs. Maria, was enjoying a cold, refreshing drink called horchata on her front porch. And on the sidewalk in front of her home, Amirah spotted a boy from school, Billy, who was walking four dogs at the same time!

"Billy!" she exclaimed, jogging over to him. "I didn't know you had four dogs! They're beautiful!"

"They're not all mine," Billy replied as he pointed to a little brown dog. "Just this one. This is Fiesta." Fiesta wagged his tail at the mention of his name. "I started a dog-walking business this summer. These other three dogs belong to some of my clients."

Amirah's eyes widened. "You started your own business?" she said. "Wow. That's amazing."

"It's okay, I guess," Billy said.

"Fiesta is such a great name for a dog," Amirah continued, bending over to let Fiesta sniff her hand. "Did you name him that because you love birthday parties?"

"Well . . ." Billy shifted uncomfortably. Amirah wasn't sure if maybe he was shy, or just in a rush to get back to work.

Before Billy could finish his sentence, a fluffy black shepherd started to pull at the leash. A roly-poly dachshund yipped and ran in a circle around Billy's legs, while the chihuahua pulled the leash in another direction. Soon they were all tangled up—including Billy!

Amirah would've giggled, but Billy's face had fallen into a frustrated frown. "Here—let me help—" she said, not wanting him to feel even more embarrassed.

"It's fine," Billy said shortly. "It happens more than you think."

Then, with a heavy sigh, he began to patiently untangle the dogs' leashes.

"Amirah!" Mama called from the driveway, jingling her keys. "Let's go!"

"See you later," Amirah told Billy. Then, with a quick wave, she hurried over to her mom's car.

Amirah was quiet while they drove to the market. Billy didn't seem to think his dog-walking business was a big deal, but Amirah thought it was incredible. *Maybe I'll start a business of my own someday,* she thought dreamily. *A cake-baking business. Or a—a birthday business!*

Amirah wasn't entirely sure what a birthday business would be like, but she knew she had plenty of time to figure it out.

"Amir and I are going to get some groceries for dinner," Mama told Amirah when they reached the store. "Why don't you grab what you need and meet us at the checkout counter?"

"You got it," Amirah replied. "Thanks again!"

Amirah could've found her way to the baking aisle blindfolded. After all, it was her favorite aisle in the entire store! But when she reached it, she noticed right away that something was different. There were empty spaces on the shelves, spaces that should've held tubs of frosting and sacks of sugar and—

Amirah stared in disbelief.

Where were the *sprinkles*?

The shelf that normally held sprinkles— jar after jar of sprinkles in every color (not to mention Amirah's favorite, rainbow sprinkles all jumbled up together)—was completely bare.

The hollowness of the gray steel shelves left Amirah feeling empty inside too. She had never seen the decorating section of the baking aisle like this before.

Maybe—maybe a lot of people are celebrating summer birthdays, she thought, trying to look on the bright side. *Maybe a delivery truck will pull up first thing tomorrow morning filled with cases of sprinkles and sugar!*

With one last look at the empty shelves, Amirah turned away from the baking aisle and made her way to the party supplies aisle, another favorite spot in the store. But today, that was where she got another unpleasant surprise: The shelves were as empty as in the baking aisle, and the supplies that were still left had been roughly scattered around. Some had even fallen on the floor.

This is terrible! Amirah thought as she knelt down to pick up some packages of birthday cake candles. There was a dented cardboard crown on the floor too; she tried to straighten it before she put it back on the shelf, but Amirah could already tell that it would never look shiny and new again.

It's bad enough that all of the party supplies are cleaned out, Amirah thought. *But everything*

being such a mess too? There's no excuse for that!

Despite the disarray, Amirah had slightly better luck searching through the party supplies. There was one package of sparkly pink candles left, and it contained just enough candles for Paulina's cake. Amirah held tightly on to it as she went to the front of the store to meet her mother and brother.

"Did you find everything you need?" Amirah asked her mother.

"Oh yes," Mama said, showing Amirah her basket, which was brimming with fresh fruits and vegetables. "How about you?"

"Not really," Amirah said dejectedly. "I got the right kind of candles, at least. But the cake decorations were all sold out."

"I'm sorry," Mama replied. "But don't lose hope, princess. I know you'll think of something just as special for Paulina's cake."

I hope so, Amirah thought.

CHAPTER TWO

BEFORE BED THAT NIGHT, Amirah reached for her favorite book. It wasn't a novel or a storybook, but a cookbook—a very special cookbook—that Mrs. Maria had given her six months ago: *The Power of Sprinkles.*

It was, Amirah suspected, the cookbook that had started it all.

That's where she had found a special birthday cake recipe with her name on it, which was a big surprise. Amirah loved her name, which meant "princess," but it was unusual enough that she rarely saw it in print.

The Power of Sprinkles also had unique recipes for all her B-Buds' favorite birthday cakes. Amirah couldn't help smiling as she thought about Mei and Elvis and Olivia. But just as quickly, the memory of the empty shelves at the store came back to her, and Amirah's smile started to fade. More than anything, she wished she could see her B-Buds and tell them about it.

To cheer herself up, Amirah started turning the pages of the old cookbook. No matter how gentle she was, some of the gold binding flaked off in her hands. That wasn't the most unusual thing about this book. The first time she had turned these pages, a cloud of sparkles that only Amirah could see had appeared, dancing and twinkling up her fingers, up her hand, up her arm—an early sign of the magic within.

That didn't happen much anymore, though, but Amirah wasn't worried. She knew the cookbook was just as powerful as ever.

It had been a busy day, but not just that—it had been a day of roller-coaster emotions. And the heat was so tiring. No wonder Amirah was exhausted, flipping through the cookbook in a dreamlike state as the crickets sang their night-time song outside her window.

Amirah covered her mouth as she yawned. She'd go to bed soon—she'd fall asleep, whether she wanted to or not—but not just yet. She still had to read over the recipe for Mei's birthday cake, a strawberry shortcake with sugar-syrup-soaked sponge cake that was practically bursting with juicy berries. Amirah licked her lips. As she read over the ingredients, she could almost taste them—sugar, cream, vanil—

Wait. The word . . . it was . . . it was fading . . . right before her eyes . . .

No . . . all the words . . . the entire recipe . . . disappearing . . .

"No!" Amirah cried, powerless to stop the recipe from vanishing. Frantically, she grabbed the page, as if her fingers could hold the words there before they disappeared for good.

And then, just like magic, they were back: each and every word, exactly as it had been before. Not a single letter out of place.

Amirah's heart was thudding in her chest as she stared at the page. *That did* not *just happen,* she thought. *Printed recipes in cookbooks don't disappear. It's not possible. I must have dozed off . . .*

I was probably having one of those dreams where you don't know you're dreaming . . .

But Amirah knew that she had been very much awake.

Gently—almost tenderly—she closed the cookbook and slid it under her pillow. She didn't want to be separated from *The Power of Sprinkles*, not after what had just happened—or what she thought had just happened.

As Amirah rested her head on her rainbow-striped pillowcase, she fell into a deep, restless sleep.

And this time, she dreamed.

◇ ◆ ◇

IN HER DREAM, Amirah blinked—once, then twice—as a grin spread across her face. "I'm back," she whispered joyfully. "I'm back!"

The Magical Land of Birthdays stretched all around her, as far as she could see. But as Amirah looked around, her smile began to fade. She was in the Magical Land of Birthdays again—there was no doubt about that—but it wasn't quite as enchanting as she remembered.

In fact, it wasn't very enchanting at all.

Amirah's nose wrinkled as she caught the scent of burned birthday cake drifting by on the breeze. She'd only smelled it once before, when an unexpected visitor prevented Mama from taking a cake out of the oven in time, but the harsh, charred smell was one she'd never forget.

A heavy mist—mixed with a tinge of smoke—hung over the land, making the once-brilliant colors appear washed out and faded. The colorful cake pops lining the path made a sorry sight as their frosting oozed to the ground in fat, greasy droplets. Helium balloons in the sky began to droop, as if each one had sprung a leak at the exact same time. The streamers that decorated each tree had lost all their festiveness, flopping from the branches as if they'd been caught in a bad storm.

A storm.

Just as the word popped into Amirah's head, a gust of smoky wind picked up. It whipped her hair around her face, and she quickly twisted it into a messy bun at the back of her head—just in time to see something: a faded scrap of paper carried on the wind.

Instinctively, Amirah wanted to know what it was.

It fluttered to the ground a few feet away, so Amirah left the path to pick it up. The soft green grass that she remembered growing in the Magical Land of Birthdays was dry and brittle now. It crunched under her feet and turned to powder with every step she took.

She approached the piece of paper cautiously.

Don't be so silly, Amirah told herself. *It's just a piece of paper. It can't hurt you.*

Soon she was close enough to see that there was something written on it. Could it be a message—a message for *her*? This wouldn't be the first time the Magical Land of Birthdays had tried to tell her something.

Something told Amirah that it was important. But still, for some reason, she hesitated. Just as Amirah reached out her hand—

Whoosh!

Another sudden gust of wind picked up the paper and carried it farther away!

Amirah frowned. Now she was determined—completely and utterly determined—to read whatever was written on the paper. She didn't dawdle this time. Instead, Amirah scrambled over the rocky hillside. Soon she was close enough to see the word BIRTHDAY written on the paper in bold, blocky handwriting. She reached out again and—

Whoosh!

This is getting ridiculous, Amirah thought as, once again, the paper fluttered just out of reach, landing in the crook of a wizened old tree. She raced the wind to reach it, hoping against hope that the tree's rough bark would somehow keep it there until she could reach it. The wind was blowing harder now. It almost seemed to be pushing her forward, faster, faster, faster—until suddenly, there she was, standing in the shadow of the gnarled tree.

The snippet of paper, still stuck in the tree, was just out of her reach.

Amirah took a deep breath, crouched down low, and leaped into the air. Her fingers brushed the edge of the paper. She grabbed and grasped and closed her hand around it in a tight fist. Amirah didn't trust that wind, with its eerie mist and stench of smoke. She wouldn't let it take the paper away from her again.

Amirah was so eager to see what the paper had to say that her hands trembled a little as she unfolded it.

"An invitation!" she exclaimed, speaking aloud even though there was no one to hear her. It was in pretty bad shape, though. The bottom half of the birthday party invitation was missing, and it almost looked like it had been clawed or shredded. The color was faded to a muted, splotchy grayish red. She couldn't tell whose party it was, or where it was supposed to be held. Besides the heading, which read YOU'RE INVITED TO A BIRTHDAY PARTY!, the only other part Amirah could read was the date—July 8, almost exactly one year ago.

Maybe that was why the invitation was in such bad shape. The party had happened a long time ago.

Or, Amirah thought, maybe there was another reason.

Just like that, the invitation—or what was left of it—crumbled into sparkly dust in her hands.

"No!" Amirah cried. But it was too late.

The invitation was gone.

She sighed heavily and looked around the empty landscape. That was when she realized the most unusual thing about the Magical Land of Birthdays: the silence. There was no laughter, no music, no happy birthday song. Just empty, hollow silence that blanketed the land as thoroughly as the mist.

Amirah decided to climb the rest of the way up the hillside. It wasn't very far. She hoped, at the top of the hill, she might be able to see more of her favorite place. Maybe she'd even be able to figure out where that burned smell was coming from.

At the top of the hill, Amirah finally realized where she was. It was an area of the Magical Land of Birthdays that she'd never visited before—but she'd seen it on a map, and knew she'd never forget it.

Sparkle City.

With the smoky mist growing thicker by the minute, Amirah didn't want to venture into that unfamiliar city all alone. She wished—and not for the first time—that her B-Buds were with her.

Then, in a flash of inspiration, she suddenly realized that she wouldn't have to go alone. Cara the Unicorn lived in the Magical Land of Birthdays! Amirah and Cara had shared a special bond from the moment they met, when Cara was stuck in piñata form and Amirah had freed her. They'd traveled the length of the Magical Land of Birthdays and back again. No matter what, Amirah knew, Cara would always come when Amirah needed her.

"Cara!" Amirah's voice echoed off the buildings as if the city were calling for Cara too. "Cara!"

Amirah didn't just listen for hoofbeats; she pressed her palms against the ground, hoping to feel it vibrating as Cara's golden hooves thundered across the land. But the silence stretched on. Amirah called for Cara again and again, but there was no sign that the unicorn heard her.

Amirah stood up, wrapped her arms around herself, and shivered—even though the day wasn't particularly cold. There was no way for her to deny it any longer.

No one was coming.

Not her B-Buds.

Not even Cara.

CHAPTER THREE

WITH A GASP, Amirah bolted upright. She rubbed her eyes, and it took her a moment to realize that she was in her bed, in her room, in her house. The Magical Land of Birthdays was gone.

It was just a dream, she realized in relief. But why did it feel so real?

Was it because she'd been so upset about the missing birthday invitations?

Was it somehow connected to the way the words in *The Power of Sprinkles* seemed to disappear right before her eyes?

What did it all mean?

Amirah shook her head, as if to shake away the last cobwebs of sleepiness and focus on the day that had just begun. She might not understand what her dream meant . . . and maybe it didn't mean anything at all. But she had a birthday cake to bake—and just the thought filled her with excitement!

Amirah hopped out of bed and changed

into her favorite baking outfit: bright pink overalls and sky-blue high-top sneakers. She twisted
a rainbow-striped scarf around her head so that
her bouncy curls wouldn't get in her face. And
just like that, she was ready for her day!

Amirah bounded downstairs to the kitchen,
where her parents, Mama and Baba, were
enjoying their morning coffee. "Let's get cook-
ing!" she exclaimed as she opened the fridge
and started pulling out the cold ingredients
she'd need: butter, eggs, milk.

Mama and Baba exchanged a grin.

"Aren't you forgetting something?" Mama
asked.

"Oops!" Amirah giggled. "Good morning!"
She hurried over to give her parents a hug and
kiss.

"Good morning to you too," Baba teased
Amirah.

"Thanks," Mama said. "But what I meant
was . . . breakfast!"

"Right! I guess I forgot that too," Amirah replied.

"Let's have quesadillas with fresh salsa," Mama suggested as she stood up from the table. "By the time we finish eating, the butter will be softened—"

"And we can start mixing Paulina's cake!" Amirah finished for her.

Mama was right, of course. By the time breakfast was over and the dishes washed and stacked in the drying rack, the butter was just squishy enough for mixing.

"Let's get baking," Amirah cheered.

"I can't wait to see how this turns out," Mama said as they got to work.

The cake itself was fairly simple because Amirah was sticking to classic flavors that she knew Paulina would love—sweet vanilla cake with creamy vanilla frosting. But that was where the simplicity ended. The design Amirah had in mind for Paulina's cake was truly spectacular, and like Mama, she couldn't wait to see how it was going to turn out.

After the cakes cooled, Amirah carefully cut a hole into the center of each layer. In this way, Paulina's cake was similar to Amirah's own unicorn birthday cake in that it would have a hole running through the center of it, top to bottom, once the layers were stacked. But this hole wasn't going to be filled with sprinkles like Amirah's special cake was. No, this cake was going to have a doll stuck into the hole in the center, up to her waist, so her torso, head, and shoulders peeked out the top of the cake.

Amirah carefully shaped the cake to look like the skirt of a poufy dress and then iced and decorated it to look like the bottom half of a princess dress. With the doll poking out of the center, the overall effect was of a beautiful doll cake.

"I think you've outdone yourself with this one," Mama commented as she admired the finished cake. "It looks so beautiful!"

"I think she's going to love it." Amirah grinned.

Mama gestured to the extra cake batter left in the bowl on the counter. "What do you want to do with the leftover batter?"

Amirah knew exactly what she wanted to do with it!

"Mini cakes!" she cried. And sure enough, there was enough batter left over to make four mini cakes.

While she waited for the mini cakes to bake, Amirah put Paulina's cake in the fridge to give the beautiful frosting a chance to set. A brief image of the drippy cake pops from her dream flitted through her mind, but Amirah pushed the thought away. She was not going to let that happen to Paulina's special cake!

At last, Amirah—and the cake—were ready to go. She placed Paulina's cake in a tall box and tied a shimmery pink ribbon around it with a big, poufy bow on top.

In the car, Mama drove slowly and carefully, avoiding every bump in the road. Amirah used her legs to hold the cake perfectly still on the floor in the back seat of the car. She couldn't wait to see the look on Paulina's face when she peeked inside the cake box!

"What if she's not home?" Amirah asked Mama. "I should've called first!"

"If she's not home, we'll take the cake back to the fridge and try again later," Mama assured her.

Amirah didn't need to worry, though. Paulina was relaxing in a hammock with a book when they arrived at her house.

"Amirah!" Paulina exclaimed happily. "What are you doing here?"

"Happy birthday!" Amirah sang out. She presented the cake box to Paulina. "I have something special for you."

Paulina's eyes brightened. "Is that what I think it is?" she asked in excitement.

Mama and Amirah exchanged a secret smile. No matter what Paulina was imagining, Amirah was confident she couldn't guess it was an extra-special cake that Amirah had created just for her.

"Open it!" Amirah encouraged her.

"Open it inside," Mama added.

"Yes! Out of this hot sun," Amirah said with a laugh.

"Now this is getting even more mysterious," Paulina said. She led Amirah and her mother into the kitchen, where she placed the tall box on the counter. Paulina's finger touched the silky ribbon. "It's almost too pretty to open," she said.

"Trust me, what's inside is even better," Amirah told her.

Paulina grinned at her friend, then held one end of the ribbon out to Amirah. "Let's do it together," she suggested. "On the count of three. One, two . . ."

"Three!" both girls said at the same time as

they each tugged on a different end of the ribbon. The poufy bow melted away as the ribbon slid off the box. Paulina lifted the lid and peeked inside. Her gasp of astonishment was better than Amirah had imagined.

"Oh, Amirah!" Paulina breathed. "This can't be a cake! It's too beautiful! Way too beautiful to eat!"

"Trust me, it's going to taste even better than it looks," Amirah said. "And the doll is yours to keep after you finish the cake—she's the other part of your present!" Then Amirah reached out to give Paulina a big hug. "Happy birthday! I'm so sorry I missed your party."

Paulina waved her hand in the air like it was no big deal. "That's okay," she said. "It's not your fault that you didn't get the invitation. And guess what? You weren't the only one."

"Really?" Amirah asked.

Paulina nodded. "Yeah, three other people

never got their invitations either," she said, sighing.

"That's so weird," Amirah said. "What do you think happened?"

"I have no idea," Paulina replied. "They were all addressed and stamped the same way. I left them all in my mailbox for the letter carrier to take. I can't explain why some of the invitations were delivered and some of them just . . . disappeared."

Amirah was quiet. She didn't have an explanation either.

"But next year I'm going to take them all to the post office," Paulina declared. "Or maybe I'll even hand-deliver them."

"Hand delivery! That will guarantee that each invitation gets where it needs to go," Amirah agreed.

"And you know what my mother said?" Paulina asked. "That maybe the invitations just got delayed! She said sometimes the mail is late."

Amirah's eyes went wide. It would be pretty frustrating to get a party invitation after the party had already happened . . . but at least that would solve the mystery of where her invitation was.

"Thank you so much for this beautiful cake," Paulina continued. "It's so special."

"Just like you," Amirah told her friend. "Happy birthday again. Next year, we will definitely celebrate in style!"

"Definitely!" Paulina said.

◆ ◇ ◆

WHEN MAMA AND AMIRAH got home, Amir had a stack of books for them to read together. "First, some lemonade," Mama told him. "That way our throats won't get too dry."

Amirah licked her lips. Mama was right, as usual. A cold glass of sweet lemonade would be perfect on such a hot summer day.

"I'll squeeze the lemons!" Amir exclaimed as he scampered toward the kitchen.

"I'll be right there to help," Amirah told him.

Just then, Amirah heard a scratching noise outside the front door, and the unmistakable *squeeeeeak* of the mailbox opening. Amirah loved to get the mail—she never knew what surprises might be waiting in the mailbox—and today, with Paulina's words about late-delivered mail fresh in her mind, she was more eager than ever to check. So eager, in fact, that she didn't even wait for the letter carrier to finish before she swung the front door open wide.

"Oh!" Amirah exclaimed in surprise. It wasn't the letter carrier at their mailbox. It was Billy, looking just as surprised as Amirah felt. Three small dogs sat at his feet, their leashes all tangled up.

"Hi, Billy," Amirah said. "What are you doing? I mean, what are you doing here?"

Billy's mouth opened, then closed before he said a word. Then he tried again. "I'm delivering flyers. For my dog-walking business," he said. He shuffled from one foot to the other, then pressed a flyer into Amirah's hand. "Here."

Amirah looked at the flyer, still surprised that Billy was at her mailbox. "But—we don't have a dog," she said.

"Oh," Billy replied. "Well, maybe you can give it to somebody who does."

He knelt down to untangle the leashes, making his dark hair fall across his eyes. "Bye," Billy said. Then, with all the dogs yipping and yapping, Billy set off down the path to the sidewalk.

Amirah stepped back into the cool living room and stared at the flyer. It was printed on red paper, with a cartoon drawing of a dog in thick black ink. Familiar, and yet not . . . almost as if she'd seen it in a dream . . .

The Power of Sprinkles popped into Amirah's mind just then. She stared at the flyer, but the words stayed steady. The letters didn't tremble and fade. Of course they didn't.

But Amirah just couldn't shake the feeling that all of it was somehow connected.

"Mama?" she called. "I think I want to bring one of the little cakes to Mrs. Maria."

"Good idea!" Mama's voice carried to Amirah from the kitchen. "She'll love a sweet treat on such a hot day. And when you get back, we'll have a tall glass of lemonade waiting for you."

"Thanks, Mama. Thanks, Amir," Amirah replied. In the kitchen, she put the little cake on its own plate and then left for Mrs. Maria's house.

She wasn't sure why she felt such a sense of urgency to visit Mrs. Maria. But Amirah knew she couldn't wait.

CHAPTER FOUR

MRS. MARIA WAS one of Amirah's best friends and quite possibly her favorite neighbor. She lived just down the street and was always happy to have a visit from Amirah. She loved to cook just as much as Mama and Amirah did, and the smell of spices in her kitchen—oregano and chilis, cinnamon and anise—was such a familiar and friendly smell that it always made Amirah feel right at home.

Rap-rap-thud-thud-tap-tap-tap! Mrs. Maria had told Amirah many times that she could stop by anytime—no need to call first—but Amirah's special knock always told her she was there.

Sure enough, Mrs. Maria was already grinning when she opened the door.

"What a special surprise on such a steamy day!" Mrs. Maria cried. "Come in out of the heat!"

"And here's another surprise!" Amirah said as she held out the little cake. It didn't seem possible, but Mrs. Maria's smile grew even bigger.

"Mmm, how beautiful! You'll split it with me, I hope," Mrs. Maria told her.

"I'll just have a bite . . . or three," Amirah replied with a grin.

"And how about some nice cold horchata?" Mrs. Maria suggested.

"Perfect!" Amirah replied.

A few minutes later, Amirah and Mrs. Maria sat across from each other with plates of cake and glasses of horchata. The sweet, creamy horchata was flecked with cinnamon. It was cool and refreshing, the perfect drink to accompany the cake Amirah had made.

"Mmm," Amirah said happily, wiping her mouth after she took a big sip of her horchata.

Mrs. Maria smiled. "Some people only like to have cinnamon during the cooler months, but I like it every day of the year," she said in a voice that sounded like she was telling Amirah a big secret.

"Me too," Amirah replied.

"And cake, of course," Mrs. Maria continued, her eyes twinkling. "I could eat cake every day of the year too. Especially one as delicious as this one. Tell me, my dear, where did you get this recipe? From one of your cookbooks?"

"Not exactly," Amirah replied. "It's our favorite vanilla cake recipe. But, speaking of cookbooks . . ."

"Go on," Mrs. Maria encouraged her.

Amirah sighed. She didn't know where to begin. So she jumped right in and hoped that Mrs. Maria wouldn't laugh. "It's about *The Power of Sprinkles*," she said. And with just those words, the whole story tumbled out—from the missing invitations to the empty shelves at the store to the way the words seemed to fade on the page to Amirah's troubling dream.

"It's almost—like—like—there's something wrong in the birthday universe," Amirah struggled to explain. "I feel like I have to fix it, but I don't know how."

Mrs. Maria didn't laugh. As Amirah looked at her friend's face, all wrinkled with concern, she knew that that was something she didn't need to worry about. Not ever.

"I can tell that your heart is troubled," Mrs. Maria finally said. "I could tell it from the moment I opened the door and saw you standing there with this pretty little cake."

Amirah nodded as she took another sip of horchata. Of course Mrs. Maria already knew something was bothering her. Sometimes she just seemed to know things like that—even before Amirah could tell her.

"What do you think I should do?" Amirah asked. "I feel like I have to go back."

"Go back?" Mrs. Maria asked, raising an eyebrow.

"To the Magical Land of Birthdays," Amirah tried to explain. "Something's wrong, and I need to make it right. My birthday's not for six whole months, though. And I don't want to wait that long! I don't know if I can!"

"No," Mrs. Maria said thoughtfully. "When there are troubles weighing on your heart, every minute that passes feels like an eternity."

Amirah smiled gratefully. Somehow, some way, Mrs. Maria always understood. And she always knew just what to say.

"So what should I do?" Amirah asked again.

"You must trust your heart, of course," Mrs. Maria told her. "You're already listening to it— that's why you feel these troubles so intensely. But here is the secret . . ."

As Mrs. Maria's voice dropped to a hush, Amirah leaned forward until she was sitting on the edge of her chair.

"You *have* to believe," Mrs. Maria continued. "You still believe in the magic of birthdays, yes?"

"Of course!" Amirah replied. "I'll *always* believe in it."

Mrs. Maria nodded, satisfied. "Then if you believe in birthday magic, and you follow your heart, you will figure out what to do," she promised Amirah.

Amirah was so lost in thought that initially, she didn't answer. Then an idea came to her . . . shadowy and half formed at first, but the more she thought about it, the more she understood.

Amirah stood up so fast that her chair screeched as it slid across the floor. "Thank you," she said breathlessly. She started to pick up her plate to take it to the kitchen, but Mrs. Maria rested her hand on Amirah's wrist.

"Leave it," Mrs. Maria said gently. "You do what you need to do."

Impulsively, Amirah gave Mrs. Maria a fast hug. Then she hurried out the door and ran down the sidewalk, not even noticing the blistering heat of the midafternoon sun.

She knew that she needed to get back to the Magical Land of Birthdays—there wasn't a shred of doubt in her mind about that—and she knew that she needed to go right now. Today! She couldn't wait six more months for her birthday. She didn't want to wait even one more day.

Back at home, Amirah slipped through the door so quietly that Mama and Amir didn't even hear her. She could hear Mama's voice as she read to Amir and the clinking of the ice cubes in their glasses of lemonade.

Amirah pressed her hand over her pocket. The vial of sprinkles that she carried with her—everywhere, always—was there, just as she expected. And that was a good thing, because Amirah had a feeling that it was going to take all the birthday magic she could muster *and* the power of sprinkles to transport herself back to the Magical Land of Birthdays when it definitely wasn't her birthday.

In the quiet of the kitchen, Amirah shook a rainbow of sprinkles into her hand. Then she picked just the ones she needed: pink for herself, purple for Mei, green for Elvis, blue for Olivia . . . What about yellow and orange, though? The rainbow wouldn't be complete without them.

And neither, Amirah thought, *would birthday magic.*

She carefully lined the sprinkles, one of each color, on the counter. She thought of her B-Buds and wished that she could see them.

Then Amirah closed her eyes, made a wish, and popped the sprinkles into her mouth.

Almost immediately, Amirah could feel the room spinning and the floor falling from beneath her feet. Her hands gripped the counter as she opened her eyes. Colors—colors everywhere—swirling in kaleidoscope patterns, shimmering and glimmering with magical light.

Amirah threw back her head and laughed with glee. As the colors sparkled and became almost blindingly bright, she closed her eyes again.

She knew where she'd be when she opened them.

And Amirah couldn't wait!

CHAPTER FIVE

SOON THE SPINNING began to slow, the swirling stopped, and the rainbow sparkles scattered, clearing the way for Amirah to see that she had, at last, returned to the Magical Land of Birthdays. She was so grateful to be back, even though the land was shadowed like it had been in her dream.

Suddenly, Amirah heard her name. She looked up with a start. It was Olivia!

"You're here!" Amirah cried as she ran across the clearing to give Olivia a big hug.

"Can you believe it? Back in the Magical Land of Birthdays—and it's not even our birthday," Olivia said, giggling. "Is it just us? Have you seen any of the other B-Buds?"

"Like me?" a new voice said.

Olivia and Amirah exchanged a grin. They would've known that voice anywhere.

"Elvis!" they yelled at the same time.

He stepped out of the grove with a great big grin on his face. "Happy almost–half birthday!"

he exclaimed. Then he glanced around. "Where's Mei? She's got to be here somewhere."

"I'm sure of it," Amirah replied confidently. After all, she'd chosen a special sprinkle for each one of her B-Buds. She was certain that birthday magic would make sure no one had been left behind.

"Then . . . where is she?" Olivia asked slowly.

The B-Buds glanced around the clearing. There was no sign of anyone else, which made Amirah start to wonder if something had gone wrong.

No, she told herself firmly. Birthday magic wouldn't fail them. Not like this.

"I'm up here!" Mei's voice floated down from overhead. The B-Buds immediately looked up—and spotted Mei peeking at them through the streamers that decorated a nearby tree.

Mei used her gymnastics abilities to climb

down the tree, as nimble and light-footed as a cat. When she was only a few feet off the ground, Mei dismounted and landed soundly on her feet. With a sly smile, she flung her arms into the air as if she were at the end of a gymnastics routine, making all the B-Buds laugh.

"How'd you end up in a *tree*?" Elvis finally asked, staring at the branches in astonishment.

"Birthday magic?" Mei said, making such a funny face that everyone laughed again. "No, honestly, I was having a snack before I went to gymnastics practice and I was think- ing about the balance beam routine I need to practice and I guess the circuits got a little scrambled or something."

Amirah's smile faltered for a moment as she remembered her dream, when so much had seemed so wrong in the Magical Land of Birthdays. She looked at each B-Bud's face to see if they had noticed yet. But they all seemed so happy and excited to be together again. Amirah hated to ruin their reunion with her worries.

"Hello?" a new voice said.

The B-Buds froze. They were all here—Amirah, Mei, Olivia, Elvis. So who was this?

A tall girl, her hair braided with hundreds of orange beads, approached them. A boy walking beside her was wearing a yellow hoodie. As the sun peeked around a cloud, he shrugged off the hoodie, neatly folded it, and carried it over his arm.

Orange, Amirah thought. *Yellow.* She remembered the extra sprinkles she'd been compelled to add and grinned. "Hi!" she said. "We're the B-Buds. We all have the same birthday—"

"Is today *your* birthday?" Mei asked the new kids, so excited to meet them that she didn't even notice she was interrupting.

The boy and the girl exchanged a glance, then shook their heads.

"No, no—not today," the boy replied in a crisp British accent. "We do have the same birthday, though, but it's in January."

"Let me guess," Amirah said. "January 8?"

The boy's eyes widened. "Exactly right," he said.

"How did you know that?" the girl asked. Her voice had a musical quality, the words lilting and blending together.

"Our birthday is on January 8 too," Amirah explained. "That's what makes us B-Buds. I just had a funny feeling that you two were also B-Buds! I'm Amirah, and that's Mei, and that's Olivia, and over there—that's Elvis."

"Cool. Thanks," the boy replied. "My name's Ziggy, and this is Lacey, but I gotta ask you—what is a B-Bud, exactly?"

"It's short for 'birthday buddy,'" Amirah

explained. "We all met here on our eleventh birthday last January. I don't know why you weren't here. We always felt like someone was missing. The carousel had space for six . . ."

Lacey and Ziggy exchanged another glance. "But we *were* here," Lacey said. "Not"—she paused to hold out her arms—"right *here*. But *here*, in the Magical Land of Birthdays. Ziggy and I celebrated together in Sparkle City."

Sparkle City? Amirah gasped, recognizing the name and the place from her dream. She also remembered seeing Sparkle City on the map she and her B-Buds had found during their last visit.

"That's right," Ziggy added, nodding his head. "We spent the whole day exploring it. It was wild! Our only regret was that we never made it out of the city to see what else is in the Magical Land of Birthdays."

"Well, it looks like it's your lucky day," Elvis joked. "We can take you on a grand tour—the

Rainbow Forest, Celebration Shore, Candle Cave, the Party Hat Mountains . . ."

"Yes, yes, yes, and yes!" Ziggy said enthusiastically. "Lead the way!"

Elvis set off with all the B-Buds following along behind him. Mei wrinkled up her face. "Look at all that trash!" she said, pointing at some scraps of faded red paper. "Yuck! I hate litterbugs."

"Maybe it blew away from somebody's party and they didn't notice," Amirah said. "Or maybe it was confetti! I love confetti but it goes *everywhere*. One time I had all this confetti at my birthday party, and even though I cleaned up afterward, I was still finding confetti for months and months!"

She paused to pick up the trash, then shoved it in her pockets. The other B-Buds helped too.

"Better already," Amirah said, smiling.

"So how did you all get here?" Lacey asked. "For us, it was our birthday cakes."

"You have birthday cake even when it's not your birthday?" Olivia asked in surprise. "What a great idea!"

Lacey laughed as she shook her head. "No, I meant last January," she explained. "It was magical! One bite of my special coconut birthday cake and *poof*! I found myself in the most wonderful city I'd ever seen in my life!"

"That's how it happened for me too," Ziggy spoke up. "Except my cake was a caterpillar cake. Best birthday cake I've ever had!"

As soon as Ziggy said the words *caterpillar cake*, a memory popped into Amirah's head. The very first time she dreamed of the Magical Land of Birthdays, before she met her B-Buds, Amirah had seen a caterpillar cake rush past her. She was almost positive that she'd heard the cake mumble something about how it was looking for someone named Ziggy.

"Was your caterpillar cake fudge on the

inside, with tiny chocolate shoes and a white chocolate face?" Amirah asked.

"How did you know that?" Ziggy gasped. "Is your special birthday cake a caterpillar cake too?"

Amirah explained how she had encountered Ziggy's cake on her last visit.

"It sounds like this place might be even more magical than we realized!" Olivia commented.

"So how did everyone get here *today*?" Amirah asked.

"I had just taken a bite of a sugar cookie," Olivia said. "With blue frosting and plenty of hundreds and thousands, of course."

Amirah grinned at Olivia. It didn't matter that Amirah called them sprinkles or that Olivia called them hundreds and thousands: They were definitely magical!

"I had a donut," Elvis said. "You know that bad boy was loaded up with sprinkles. It had so many sprinkles on it I couldn't even see if the frosting was chocolate or vanilla!"

"I had ice cream!" Mei said excitedly. "And the cone had been dipped in chocolate and rolled in rainbow sprinkles. How about you, Amirah?"

"Sprinkles, of course," she replied. "I made sure to choose one in each color—pink, yellow, orange, green, blue, and purple."

"The rainbow!" Olivia suddenly exclaimed.

Everyone turned to look at her.

"Put us together, and our favorite colors make the rainbow," she explained. "See?"

And now that she'd mentioned it, it was unmistakable. Even in their regular clothes, the B-Bud's favorite colors shone through. There was a completeness to their group that had been missing last January—even though Amirah hadn't known what was missing until they were finally all together.

"Yes," she said, nodding. "One special

color, one special sprinkle, for each of us . . . even though I didn't know you yet, Ziggy and Lacey. I'm not surprised it was sprinkles that brought us all together. That's just the power of sprinkles at work, I guess!"

"The power of sprinkles?" Lacey asked, her eyes wide. "I've never heard of that before. I thought it was just birthday magic."

"You're not wrong," Amirah said, trying to find the right words. "They're definitely connected. I'm just not sure how."

"I don't need to know how," Lacey said with a warm smile. "Sometimes you just have to believe."

You just have to believe.

Amirah shivered. Weren't those the exact words that Mrs. Maria had said to her?

The connection that Amirah had always felt with her B-Buds had only grown stronger.

"Here's what I can't figure out, though," Ziggy said. "How come we celebrated our birthdays in the city while you celebrated yours in the countryside?"

As Ziggy spoke, Amirah's mind continued to churn:

The power of sprinkles.

Birthday magic.

They're definitely connected.

Amirah held up one hand. "Wait a second," she said, her voice low and urgent.

Everyone turned to look at her.

"Has anyone noticed . . . something wrong with birthday magic?" she began. "Back home there are some things that just—they just aren't right."

Everyone listened quietly as Amirah told them what she'd noticed since her phone call with Paulina.

"Now that you mention it . . ." Mei said. "Every year, my oba-chan—who loves birthdays as much as I do—plans a special dinner for the whole family to celebrate her birthday.

But last month, when it was her birthday, she just didn't feel like a big celebration—or any celebration," Mei finally finished with a sad shrug. "She said, 'maybe next year.'"

Amirah shook her head in sorrow. Imagine taking a year off from celebrating your birthday—the most special day of your life, the day when you were born! It was unthinkable.

"It must be an epidemic," Elvis said, his voice sounding quieter than usual.

Everyone turned to look at him.

"In my town, we had a restaurant that's all about birthdays. It's called the Birthday Cakery," he explained. "Every single room had a different party theme. You could have a dinosaur party or an art party or a princess party or a pirate party or a music party or—"

"Was there a sprinkles room?" Amirah asked brightly, holding up her vial of sprinkles and giving it a little shake.

"You know what? There was a rainbow

room with sprinkles painted on the walls," Elvis replied with a grin. Then his smile faded and he sighed. "But the Birthday Cakery went out of business three months ago," he finished. "I still can't believe it."

"Out of business?" Amirah echoed in shock. "How is that possible? That sounds like the most amazing party place on earth!"

"It was," Elvis said, nodding sadly. "But now it's gone, and all we have left are memories, I guess."

"Something weird happened in my family too," Ziggy spoke up. "On my little sister's birthday, we accidentally—we accidentally burned her cake."

Amirah's hands flew up to her face. "Oh no," she gasped.

Ziggy nodded glumly. "It was so weird—the timer never went off! And since we were outside, by the time we noticed the awful smoky smell, it

was way too late. The cake was burned black all over. We couldn't save any of it."

"Was your sister's birthday ruined?" Olivia asked.

Amirah almost didn't want to know the answer.

"Not exactly ruined," Ziggy replied. "We went out for dessert instead and we sang the birthday song at the restaurant and she seemed happy enough. But it wasn't the same. You know what I mean?"

Amirah nodded. She knew what Ziggy meant. "Something is definitely going on," she announced. "And I think—I think we've come here to fix it."

"Really?" Mei asked.

"I just have this feeling," Amirah replied.

Mei, Elvis, and Olivia exchanged a knowing look. When Amirah had a feeling about something, they took it *very* seriously.

"Tell us," Amirah said suddenly as she turned to Ziggy and Lacey. "Tell us all about Sparkle City. Everything you can remember! What it looked like, sounded like, smelled like—"

"Smelled like?" Elvis cracked in a funny voice.

But Amirah wasn't joking around. "Everything," she repeated.

"It was glorious," Lacey said, searching for the right words. Then she shook her head and shrugged. "And utterly indescribable."

Amirah understood. Some things in the Magical Land of Birthdays had to be seen to be believed.

"I think that's where we need to go," Amirah said.

"But why?" Ziggy asked. "Just curious. Why back to Sparkle City? There were no troubles there. But the countryside—well, I don't want to criticize, but it's seen better days, hasn't it? Look—there's more trash over there."

"Yes," Amirah acknowledged, bending down to pick up more scraps of paper. "And maybe Sparkle City has too. See, I have this theory..."

The other B-Buds stepped closer to her.

"What's going wrong in the Magical Land of Birthdays isn't new," Amirah said. "In fact, I think it's been happening for a while. I think it's why you two landed in Sparkle City while the rest of us were in the countryside. I think it's why Ziggy's cake was confused about not being able to find Ziggy. What if we were supposed to meet six months ago? What if we were supposed to spend our birthday together—not apart?"

No one spoke.

"I've seen the countryside twice now," Amirah continued. "I know how it's changed. But I dreamed about the Magical Land of Birthdays the other night—and honestly? It was more like a warning than a dream—"

Mei shivered. "Don't say that," she whispered.

Amirah paused to wrap her arm around Mei's shoulders and give her a hug. "Don't be scared," she said. "We're in this together. We'll fix it—no matter what it takes."

Elvis glanced around. "I'd like to go to Sparkle City," he said. "I want to see everything there is to see in the Magical Land of Birthdays!"

Lacey and Ziggy exchanged a glance. "Well . . . we don't know how to get there from here," Ziggy began.

"We don't even know exactly where we are," Lacey added.

"The map!" Mei suddenly cried. She turned to Amirah. "Did you bring the map?"

"No," Amirah admitted. "I'm sorry, B-Buds. I should've thought to grab it!"

"Don't worry about it," Elvis assured her. "We'll find our way there. We'll use birthday magic if we need to."

Amirah flashed him a grateful smile. "Ready, B-Buds?" she asked.

"Lead the way!" Ziggy cheered her on.

Amirah was about to take a step when she realized that there wasn't even a path to guide them. They'd have to push their way through the dry grass . . . and hopefully not get lost along the way.

"I do remember that Sparkle City was high up," Lacey said suddenly. "It felt like we could look out and see all of the Magical Land of Birthdays spread out below us."

"Okay, then. That's where we'll start," Amirah said. Then she began to climb up the hillside.

It seemed to get hotter and hotter as they walked, and Amirah could feel her face growing red from the heat.

Suddenly Olivia spotted something. "What's that—over there?" she asked. "It looks like a pond."

Amirah caught a glimpse of it through the tall grass. The smooth, shiny surface reflected the cloudless gray sky. "Yes!" she cried. "Let's go splash around in it! Come on!"

She took off running toward the pond with the B-Buds close behind her. She could just imagine how cool and refreshing it would feel to splash in the water. But when Amirah reached it, she felt a stab of disappointment. It wasn't a pond at all. Just a shiny piece of cellophane wrapping paper that someone had left behind. *More trash*, Amirah thought in disappointment.

"Well, that's not what we were expecting," she told the B-Buds. "Oh well! At least we won't lose any time on our journey to Sparkle City. I probably would've splashed around for, like, an hour!"

"Hold on," Ziggy said, kneeling beside the cellophane to get a closer look. He peeled up the edge and pulled off a sheet of shiny cellophane with a crinkling sound—only to reveal another sheet of cellophane beneath it. Then another, and another, and another. "What do you think this is, anyway?"

"Part of a present-wrapping station?" Olivia guessed.

"But where's the tape? The scissors? The ribbon? And especially the other kinds of wrapping paper?" Mei pointed out.

"Good point," Olivia said.

Meanwhile, Ziggy kept peeling away layer after layer of cellophane. "Sorry, B-Buds," he said, peeling faster and faster. "I've got to get to the bottom of this!"

"We can all help," Elvis said.

The other B-Buds crowded around the cellophane and started peeling away sheets of it. Then, without warning, they reached the last one—and uncovered the lid to a box.

"Should we open it?" Mei asked.

"Yes," Amirah said firmly. "Absolutely!"

Mei reached forward and inched the tight-fitting lid off the box, one wiggle at a time. When it finally came off, it released a cloud of dust into the air that made all the B-Buds sneeze.

It only took Amirah a moment to realize what was inside the box.

"Treat bags!" she cried. "Party favors!"

She pulled out a few of the striped bags and passed them around.

"They've been there for a long time, huh?" Olivia asked as she traced the letter O in the dust coating her treat bag.

"Maybe they were leftovers," Amirah suggested—but even she didn't believe that. There were too many of them. It was almost like they had been prepared for a party that had never even happened.

"Ooh! Candy!" Ziggy exclaimed as he peered into his bag.

"I wouldn't eat that—" Mei began.

But it was too late. Ziggy had already

popped a piece into his mouth. Just as quickly, though, his mouth twisted into a grimace. "Yuck," he said, turning around to spit out the candy. "It's stale. These have *definitely* been sitting around for a long time."

Elvis's bag rustled as he dug around inside it. "Look what mine has," he said, holding up a tin whistle that looked awfully familiar.

Amirah's eyes lit up. She recognized it at once.

Elvis recognized the whistle too. "You want to do the honors?" he asked.

"It would be my pleasure," Amirah replied. She held the whistle to her mouth, pursed her lips, and blew.

But the whistle didn't make a sound.

"That's a pity," Lacey said. "It must be broken."

Amirah smiled mysteriously. "Just wait," she replied. Then she blew into the silent whistle again.

The silence stretched on for seconds, then minutes. Amirah was about to blow the whistle once more when she heard it—no, she felt it first. The ground beneath them started trembling to a familiar rhythm. Then all the B-Buds could hear it: the rhythmic *clip-clop, clip-clop, clip-clop* that could only be one thing.

Hoofbeats!

CHAPTER SIX

"ARE THOSE HOOFBEATS?" Lacey asked. "Are there horses in the Magical Land of Birthdays?"

"Carousel horses, yes," Amirah replied. "But unless I'm very wrong, that's—Cara!"

Amirah couldn't even finish her sentence. She was too overjoyed to see her dear friend, Cara the Unicorn, at last. The golden unicorn gleamed as brightly as the sun as she galloped toward the B-Buds.

"Cara!" Amirah cried again. She took off running toward the unicorn at full speed. As soon as she was close enough, she threw her arms around Cara's neck, burying her face in Cara's shimmering rainbow mane. The gorgeous roses that encircled Cara's gleaming horn perfumed the air.

"I've missed you so much," Amirah whispered near Cara's ear. Amirah felt so much better already. Cara would help them find Sparkle City. Cara would help them solve the mystery of why so many birthdays had gone so wrong. Cara would show them the way.

Just then, Cara trembled, as if a shiver had shaken her whole body. She pawed at the ground anxiously and looked around for—what?

Amirah didn't know. But even without words, she could tell that Cara was worried about something.

Very worried.

"I'm here now," Amirah whispered to Cara. "I want to help. I'll do anything to help."

Cara's big, dark eyes gleamed with gratitude.

"We're trying to get to Sparkle City," Amirah continued. "Can you take us there?"

Cara nodded, a quick jerk of her head that sent shimmers down her mane.

"B-Buds!" Amirah called to her friends. "Good news! Cara can take us to Sparkle City! She knows how to get there!"

"Hooray!" The B-Buds cheered. The hope was contagious.

With Cara galloping in the lead and the B-Buds running close behind her, they set off in search of Sparkle City. Amirah's eagerness to find the magical place pushed her onward, even when the path grew steep and rocky. She was only a little out of breath when, at last, they reached the ridge overlooking the city.

And what a city it was!

Even from a distance, Amirah could see how it had earned the name "Sparkle City." The buildings glittered like jewels, with faceted sides that reflected the light and, like a prism, split it into the spectrum of the rainbow. Rainbow beams spangled every surface, from the roads to the buildings. The sparkles! The colors! The joy!

"Amazing," Mei breathed.

"I've never seen anything like it," Elvis declared. "And that kind of feels like the under-statement of the year."

"It's so beautiful," Olivia said. "This must be what it's like to pass through a rainbow."

Amirah noticed, however, that Lacey and Ziggy were strangely quiet. "What do you think, B-Buds?" she asked them. "Is it the same as you remembered?"

There was a long pause before they answered.

"I . . . It's hard to say," Lacey began. "It just seems so . . . so quiet."

"Yeah," Ziggy agreed with a curt nod. "I don't hear music or laughter or—or anything, really."

With a sinking feeling, Amirah realized how right they were.

Sparkle City was utterly deserted.

"That can't be normal," she said. "It's a city! Where are all the kids? Where are all the parties?"

"There have to be *plenty* of birthdays today," Olivia said.

And every single one of the B-Buds knew she was right.

A day without a single birthday party . . . a day when *nobody* celebrated . . . the thought made Amirah feel sick. Not just sick, though. It made her even more determined to find out what was going on.

She placed her hand on Cara's back and felt, along with the warmth, a sense of strength.

"Come on," she told the B-Buds. "We won't solve this mystery standing up here, staring at Sparkle City from far away. We've got to get down there and investigate."

The other B-Buds were quiet as they set off for the last stage of their journey to Sparkle City. It was an easy walk. When they reached Sparkle City, the bejeweled buildings sat silently, almost as if they were waiting for something . . . or someone.

Amirah wondered if the city really was as deserted as it appeared. "Hello?" she called, as loudly as she dared.

Hello-hello-hello-hello-hello

The sound of her own voice, echoing off each facet of the jewel-cut buildings, gave Amirah chills. The silence, the emptiness, the *wrongness* of it all.

Suddenly, Amirah wished she could go home and forget all about the trouble in the Magical Land of Birthdays. But she already knew that wasn't possible. Besides, the trouble had already followed them home anyway, ruining the birthdays of their friends and relatives.

I believe in birthday magic, Amirah reminded herself. It was a thought she knew she needed to hold on to—no matter what happened next.

Just ahead, the road split into three directions, and Amirah turned to Cara for advice. "Which way should we go?" she asked.

The unicorn didn't hesitate. She set off on the right-hand fork at such a fast clip that the B-Buds had to scramble to keep up.

Cara didn't slow down until she'd reached an airy tent made of colorful, gauzy panels that fluttered in the breeze.

For a moment, the B-Buds stood in stunned silence. They'd never seen anything like it. The enormous tent was filled, filled to the brim, with—

"Presents!" Elvis finally yelled. He turned to face his friends with wild joy in his eyes. "Have you ever in your whole entire life seen so many *presents?*"

Tall presents, long presents, short presents, small presents, presents so big they'd need a ladder to reach the bow on the very top. Presents wrapped in boxes, presents tucked in bags, odd-shaped presents draped with golden cloth.

When Amirah glanced at the B-Buds, they were all grinning.

"Sorry," Ziggy suddenly said. "I can't resist!"

He grabbed the nearest present, gave it a gleeful shake, and ripped off the star-covered wrapping paper to reveal a telescope.

"Huh," Ziggy said. "I wonder what the rest of the presents have insi—"

His words stopped abruptly as the telescope began to crumble in his hands. A look of panic crossed Ziggy's face as he tried to hold the present together. But it was too late. The telescope dissolved into powdery ash that slipped through his fingers, no matter how hard he tried to contain it. It formed a small, shimmering pile on the floor before a gust of wind blew through the tent, scattering the remains of the present until there was no trace of it.

None of the B-Buds were smiling anymore.

"What—what just happened?" Mei asked.

"I don't know," Ziggy said miserably. "I was just holding it—I didn't mean to—"

"I think," Amirah began, "that it wasn't your present."

Everyone turned to look at her.

"Look at all these gifts," she continued. "I bet there's one for everybody in the whole wide world.

One perfect present for every person. But if you try to take one that doesn't belong to you . . ."

Amirah didn't need to finish her sentence. Everyone knew what she meant.

"I'm sorry," Ziggy said. "I'm so sorry."

"It's okay," Amirah told him. "You didn't know."

"We can't open any more gifts, though," Lacey spoke up. "It's not worth the risk."

"Definitely not," Olivia added. She glanced around warily. "I think we should get out of here. We shouldn't mess around with birthday magic that we don't understand."

"And Sparkle City is huge. There have to be plenty of other places to explore," Mei chimed in.

"But Cara brought us here for a reason," Amirah said. "Right, Cara?"

The unicorn tossed her mane and pawed at the ground, a clear yes.

"We're not just sightseeing," Amirah said.

"Something is going seriously wrong in the Magical Land of Birthdays and it's spilling over into our world too. If this tent holds the answer—or even just a clue—we've got to find it!"

"We can't just tear open presents until we find the right one," Lacey pointed out.

"I agree," Amirah said, nodding. "That would be wrong in every way. But . . . if I could find my *own* present . . ."

"There are so many of them, though," Lacey said with a worried look. "Where would you even begin?"

Amirah wasn't sure. Deep in thought, she stroked Cara's rainbow-tinged mane. And then the answer occurred to her in a flash of intuition that was as brilliant as a stroke of lighting in a storm-dark sky.

Trust your heart.

"I will," Amirah whispered, so quietly that only Cara could hear her.

Amirah took a deep breath and began to walk through the tent. She was secretly relieved when the B-Buds didn't follow her. It was almost as if they knew that Amirah would need all her concentration to succeed. It was almost as if they knew that this was a task she had to complete on her own.

What would my perfect present look like? Amirah wondered. It was a hard question to answer. When she thought about "perfect," she imagined a gorgeous cake . . . a fun afternoon with her B-Buds . . . a happy vacation with her family. Presents weren't the most important part of birthdays to Amirah. They never had been.

One perfect present for every person, she thought. If there was one thing in the whole wide world that would represent Amirah . . .

"The power of sprinkles!" she whispered.

She started roaming the aisles through the tent, moving faster and faster, knowing in her heart that she would recognize her present as soon as she spotted it.

And then she saw it: a box, big enough that she needed to hold it with both hands, wrapped in sparkly pink paper.

The large bow, which was as big as Amirah's head, was made of sprinkle-covered ribbon.

It wasn't just the sprinkles on the ribbon that told Amirah this was the perfect present for her. It was the way she felt drawn to it, as though the box contained some sort of magnet that pulled her closer . . . and closer . . . and closer . . .

When Amirah reached the box, she hesitated for just a moment. The stakes were so high. What if she was wrong? What if she accidentally opened the wrong gift . . . and made someone else's perfect present disappear forever?

Just then, Amirah felt something soft brush against her arm. She jumped in surprise, then spun around to see Cara the Unicorn standing there.

"Hi," Amirah whispered as she stroked Cara's forehead. "Did I find it? Is this the one?"

As Amirah stared into Cara's eyes, she knew the answer.

Amirah took a deep breath and picked up the present.

Her present.

It was surprisingly heavy in her hands.

Amirah slipped off the sprinkle-covered bow and unwrapped the heavy pink paper carefully so that it wouldn't tear. At last, her perfect present was revealed. It didn't crumble or turn to dust or disappear.

"My present," Amirah whispered. She looked up at Cara, her eyes shining with happiness. "It's real!"

CHAPTER SEVEN

THE STORY OF

THE MAGICAL LAND OF BIRTHDAYS

"B-BUDS!" Amirah cried. "I found it! I found my present!"

Their footsteps clattered through the tent as Elvis, Mei, Olivia, Lacey, and Ziggy raced to meet her.

"What is it?" they asked, all at the same time.

"It's a book," Amirah said, her voice filled with wonder as she stared at the cover. The image on it shifted every few seconds. First a cake . . . then a card . . . then a gift . . . then a bunch of balloons . . .

Amirah lightly traced her hand across the cover of the book. Suddenly, words began to appear where her fingers had been.

She gasped, then read: *"The Story of the Magical Land of Birthdays."*

Amirah looked up at the B-Buds. "I think this is it," she said. "The clue we've been searching for. I think we're going to find out everything we need to know."

"What are we waiting for?" Elvis asked eagerly. "Let's read it!"

Amirah and the B-Buds sat on the ground in a circle. Then Amirah opened the book.

The page was blank.

She quickly turned to the next page, only to discover it was blank too.

"They're blank," she said as she flipped from one page to the next. She looked up at her B-Buds in dismay. "It's a blank book!"

Everyone started talking at once.

"Is it a fake?"

"Is it someone else's present?"

"Maybe you're supposed to write the story of the Magical Land of Birthdays!"

"Maybe the story starts *now!*"

Amirah tried to focus. In her heart, she knew it was the right present. But she couldn't figure out why the pages were blank. There had to be a reason—

Turn the page.

The voice inside Amirah was louder than ever. She nodded, almost to herself. She would turn every page in this thick book, each and every one of hundreds of pages, until she reached the very end.

"Amirah?"

She glanced up.

"It's blank. Why do you keep turning the pages?" Mei asked.

"I don't know," Amirah said simply. "I just want to see every page—just to make sure—"

Then, suddenly, she gasped. Halfway through the book, words began to appear like magic the moment Amirah touched the page.

The Birthday Basher

She read the words aloud, her voice trembling with excitement.

"Whoa," Elvis said. "What—where—*how*—"

"The words?" Amirah asked, keeping her

fingers pressed against the page. "I don't know, honestly. It's like . . ."

Amirah's voice trailed off as she tried to find the words. "It's like the book is only going to tell us what we need to know," she finished.

"Hurry, then," Lacey urged her. "Hurry before the words disappear!"

As if on cue, all the B-Buds inched forward, eager to hear what the book would reveal.

Amirah took a deep breath and began to read.

The Birthday Basher

THERE CAME TO PASS that a boy was born with more birthday magic than anyone before him. This boy, destined to become the prince of the Magical Land of Birthdays, was filled with so much birthday magic that he brought joy to everyone around him—no matter if it was their birthday or not.

As such, he found a previously unidentified route to the Magical Land of Birthdays at an early age and became the youngest human to venture into the land. His B-Buds soon followed, one after another, as the boy's powerful birthday magic drew them forth. They forged an unbreakable birthday bond. Everyone in the land rejoiced when he was crowned the prince, for under his guidance and leadership, it was certain that birthday joy would continue to grow until each and every person was filled with it!

Then it all came crashing down. Some terrible deed, some deep disappointment, befell the prince. No longer did he love birthdays. Now he hated them, despised them, and the birthday magic within him curdled into something bitter and ugly. Though his powers continued to grow, they transformed into unhappy birthday magic, and—unbeknownst to him—unleashed a curse across all the land. It was a contagion that, left unchecked, would sap the joy and love of

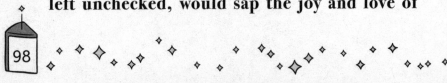

birthdays from all until birthdays themselves were forgotten.

There is but one who can stop the Birthday Basher from continuing his reign of misery, an individual who was blessed with birthday magic to rival his own. But until this individual is revealed, the Birthday Basher's ceaseless quest will continue to destroy the Magical Land of Birthdays and all birthday magic, day . . . by day . . . by day.

When Amirah finished reading, the B-Buds were quiet. The seriousness of the story weighed heavily on them. No one knew what to say— or do.

"It wasn't just our imaginations, then," Amirah finally said. "There really is something wrong in the Magical Land of Birthdays."

"Turn the page," Lacey urged her. "See if the book says anything else."

No one spoke as Amirah turned the pages,

one by one, until she reached the very end of the book. There weren't any other words. That single chapter about the Birthday Basher was all the book wanted them to know.

"I wish we had more information," Olivia said. "Who *is* this guy, anyway? How can we find him?"

"I wish we knew more about what happened to him," Amirah said. "I can't imagine anything that could make me hate birthdays."

"Did you ever think that maybe the book is trying to tell us that we *can't* stop him?" Lacey spoke up.

Everyone turned to look at her.

"I mean, it sounds like the only person who *can* stop the Birthday Basher is some kind of birthday-loving superhero with super birthday magic," she continued. "And if that's not one of us, then maybe it's saying we should go home."

"Go home?" Amirah repeated in surprise.

"You mean give up? No. I could never do that."

Lacey looked uncomfortable. "I just mean, what if this is all pointless? What if we can't do anything to fix what's happening?"

Amirah took a deep breath. Lacey was entitled to her opinion, and Amirah respected it, but she completely disagreed with what her newest B-Bud was saying.

"You don't have to stay if you don't want to," Amirah said firmly. "But I can't leave. Not now. I have to find a way to stop what's happening."

There was a long silence.

"I'm not going anywhere," Lacey said finally.

"We're your B-Buds," Mei added, and the rest of the group nodded. "We're with you all the way."

Amirah flashed her a grateful smile. "Thanks," she said. Then she absentmindedly pulled out the vial of sprinkles from her pocket. She shook a few into her hand and popped them into her mouth. The familiar sweetness swirled through her mouth as suddenly—

"Birthday cake!" she exclaimed, making all the other B-Buds jump.

"Huh?" Mei said, scrunching up her face in confusion.

Amirah leaped to her feet. "The Birthday Basher's birthday cake," she continued in a rush. "If we can find it, I think it will tell us everything we need to know. Birthday cakes are so special. So personal. They're more than just a cake. They're filled with—"

"Birthday magic," Elvis finished for her.

"Yes," Amirah said. "Exactly!"

"You don't think his cake could be in here, do you?" Olivia asked, glancing around at the towers of presents that surrounded them.

"I don't think so," Amirah said. "A birthday present isn't quite the same thing as a birthday cake."

Then she had another idea.

"Cara!" Amirah said, turning to the unicorn. "Are we on the right track? Do you know where we can find out about the Basher's favorite birthday cake?"

With a swish and swirl of her colorful mane, Cara nodded and pawed at the ground. All the B-Buds could tell she was saying yes.

Amirah placed her hand on Cara's back. "Show us the way!" she said.

CHAPTER EIGHT

THE B-BUDS HURRIED after Cara as she galloped through the streets of Sparkle City. Left, right, straight, right, straight, left—soon they felt so twisted and turned around that Amirah didn't know if they'd be able to find the present tent again if they tried.

But it was clear that Cara knew exactly where she was going, and Amirah trusted her special friend completely.

The sun had started to set, making the streets of Sparkle City glitter with golden light. It was getting late, Amirah knew. They wouldn't have much more time before nightfall.

At last, Cara came to a halt before a cavernous building. It had dozens of turrets, each one topped with a decoration that looked like a dollop of frosting. The towers at each corner resembled swirly-striped birthday cake candles, and at the very top of each one flickered a real flame.

"What is this place?" Mei asked in astonishment.

"Look," Amirah said, pointing at a sign that hung above the jeweled double doors. "It's the Hall of Birthday Cakes! Come on—let's see what's inside!"

The moment the B-Buds stepped into the Hall of Birthday Cakes, they were overcome by the most delicious scents. Chocolate, vanilla, caramel, strawberry, lemon, and sugar all combined to create a heavenly aroma.

The smell couldn't compete with the sights, though. The long corridor was lined with delicately lit glass-and-crystal cases. And inside each case was a different birthday cake!

"Look!" Olivia called. "There's a card too. It has a name and a birthday and a favorite color."

"You know what this means?" Lacey exclaimed. "*Our* birthday cakes must be in here too!"

"Do you think we can find them?" Mei asked.

"I think we should try!" Amirah replied. "There's just one question—where to begin?"

"This place is huge." Elvis spoke up. "Should we start at one end and make our way to the other?"

"That makes sense," Amirah said, nodding.

"It's gonna take us *hours* to get all the way through the entire building," Olivia said. "Maybe even *days!*"

"Then we don't have any time to lose," Amirah said.

The B-Buds walked over to the far side of the building, where Amirah spotted a small sign with ice-blue letters on it. "Look!" she cried. "January! The cakes must be arranged by month! No—by date!"

"That means our birthday will be easy to find!" Ziggy exclaimed. "Follow me!"

The B-Buds raced after Ziggy until they arrived at the section marked January 8. Even then, it wasn't as easy to find their cakes as they expected. After all, there were millions of other people who shared their special birthday around the world.

With some careful searching, though, each cake was eventually revealed. Amirah's sprinkle-filled unicorn cake, Mei's strawberry cake, Olivia's fairy bread. Then Elvis's peanut-butter-and-banana cake and Lacey's coconut cake and Ziggy's caterpillar cake!

"B-Buds, check out this cool popcorn cake," Amirah cried, pointing to a cake for someone named Nancy Gates.

"I guess that's a long-lost B-Bud of ours who really loves popcorn," Elvis commented.

"Or maybe she loves eating popcorn when she's watching TV like I do," Amirah giggled.

Birthday cakes for B-Buds born on January 8 stretched as far as the eye could see. There were even birthday cakes for famous people who shared their birthday, like David Bowie, Elvis Presley, and Stephen Hawking.

Amirah stared at her own special birthday cake. She could see her reflection smiling in the glass case that surrounded it. Just seeing the cake made her feel excited about her birthday, even though it was still six months away!

Amirah knew, though, that they didn't have time to linger. There were many more aisles left for January, followed by February and all the other months of the year.

"Should we split up?" Lacey suggested. "One B-Bud per aisle?"

Amirah nodded. "I think that's a good idea," she said. "If you find a cake that might belong to the Birthday Basher, yell and we'll all come running."

"What if we see a cake that's just really cool?" Elvis called a few minutes later. "I'm in March, and the cake for a guy named Jeffrey

Harrow, born March 29, looks just like a golf course!"

Amirah giggled but resisted the urge to go see the golf course cake. She had to focus! She raced down aisles in February and March, then April and May. Along the way, she noticed that not every glass case was filled with a beautiful birthday cake that looked too good to eat. Some of the cakes were small and slumped. Some had runny frosting that had dripped off the cakes, pooling at the bases of the pedestals. And some of them had no frosting or decoration at all. They sat there, bare and plain, looking stale and almost inedible.

Why? wondered Amirah. It didn't make sense to her why some of the birthday cakes were so grand and glorious, while others were downright disgusting. *I wonder if the way some-one feels about their birthday can affect their cake,* she thought. It seemed preposterous . . . but then again, anything was possible in the Magical Land of Birthdays.

"I'm in a June aisle!" Elvis called out. "Halfway through the year!"

"Thanks for the update!" Amirah called back—but her voice sounded a little hesitant, a little unsure. They were almost halfway through the Hall of Birthday Cakes and still had not found the Birthday Basher's cake.

What if he doesn't have a cake at all?

Amirah tried to push the idea from her mind as soon as it popped up, but it was a stubborn one. Even as it nagged at her, though, it also inspired her to search harder. And to search *smarter*.

Amirah glanced over at the nearest cake. She was still in the last week of May, but she could hear the other B-Buds had joined Elvis in combing through the June aisles.

She reached into her pocket and touched her container of sprinkles. As her fingers brushed the vial, she thought she felt it vibrate just the tiniest bit.

Amirah paused. The sprinkles were trying to tell her something. She removed the container from her pocket, unscrewed the cap, and popped a few sprinkles in her mouth.

What if I skipped June altogether? she thought as the familiar sweet taste filled her mouth. *I could leave June to the other B-Buds and go straight to July.*

Amirah knew what she had to do. She passed all the June aisles, which had an unusually large number of strawberry cakes and rose-covered cakes, and moved straight into July.

Cakes with watermelons. Cakes with cherries. Cakes with frosting fireworks and sparkler candles. She moved quickly but carefully, not wanting to miss something important. Amirah didn't want to accidentally pass by the Birthday Basher's cake—especially if, as she suspected, it might not seem as special as all the others.

As it turned out, Amirah knew it the moment she saw it. Even from ten feet away, she could tell it was the one.

Amirah almost wished that she could avoid the cake altogether. But that wasn't possible, Amirah knew. She'd made a promise to her B-Buds—and to Cara—and to the Magical Land of Birthdays itself. She didn't want to let any of them down.

So, step by step, inch by inch, Amirah crept closer.

The glass case was dark and shadowy; there were silvery cobwebs hanging from the corners. Even so, Amirah could clearly see the horrible cake that was housed inside.

At first, she thought it was covered in an unappetizing gray-green frosting topped with spun sugar. But then, with a sick feeling, she realized that fuzzy tufts of mold had spread across the cake. There was a smattering of dark wormholes along the side of the cake, and she shuddered to think what she would find if she sliced into it.

"B-Buds," she called. Then, again, a little louder. "B-Buds! I think I found it!"

She could hear their footsteps clattering through the Hall of Birthday Cakes as Mei, Elvis, Ziggy, Lacey, and Olivia hurried to join her.

"Ew!" Lacey said, wrinkling her nose. "That's *disgusting*! Are you trying to tell me it's a cake?"

"Yes," Amirah said, nodding. "Or, at least, it *used* to be a cake."

"That's the grossest thing I've ever seen," Mei said bluntly.

The rest of the B-Buds loudly agreed.

All except for Amirah. Sure, she thought the cake was gross too. But the feeling it most inspired in her wasn't disgust.

It was sadness.

How terrible, she thought sadly, *to hate your birthday so much that your cake becomes this . . . this . . . this monstrosity. How—how heartbreaking.*

Suddenly, despite all the damage he'd caused, Amirah couldn't feel angry at the Birthday Basher. Instead, she felt pity. And maybe even compassion.

That was when Amirah realized she wasn't just determined to help the Magical Land of Birthdays.

She was determined to help the Birthday Basher too.

Amirah tore herself away from the rotting cake to look for the card. It was shrunken and smudged, but she could still read it:

BILLY BONILLA
July 8
Born in Mexico
Red

Amirah gasped. She knew that name. And the Billy she knew lived in Mexico.

It couldn't be a coincidence . . . could it?

"Amirah?" Lacey asked, placing a hand on Amirah's arm. "Are you okay?"

"Um, yeah," Amirah said. "I just—I think I know him."

"You *know* him?" Elvis exclaimed. "You *know* the Birthday Basher?"

Amirah nodded. "I think he's my neighbor," she replied. "But I have to go home to check. I can't remember his exact birthday, but I know I've got it written down."

"You have your neighbor's birthday written down?" Olivia asked in surprise.

Amirah grinned at the B-Buds. "I write down everybody's birthday," she said.

Elvis stuck out his hand. "Hi, I'm Amirah," he said, pretending to introduce himself. "When's your birthday?"

All the B-Buds laughed—especially Amirah!

Just then, the low lights in the Hall of Birthday Cakes went out—all at the same time. The B-Buds were plunged into darkness, their laughter turning into shrieks.

"I guess the Hall of Birthday Cakes is closing," Mei said.

"How are we going to find our way back to the entrance?" Olivia asked, sounding worried.

"I have a light on my watch," Ziggy said. "If I could just find the right button to push . . ."

The B-Buds waited in the darkness while Ziggy fiddled with his watch. Then, suddenly, a thin beam of light shone out of the screen. It wasn't much, but it was enough for them to find their way through the long corridors back to the entrance.

Cara was waiting outside, just where they'd left her. Even in the growing darkness, though, Amirah could tell that she was anxious.

"It's okay," she whispered close to Cara's ear. "We're getting closer to fixing everything. I'm sure of it."

Cara whinnied softly, and Amirah reached out and gave her a hug. Then she turned to the B-Buds. "We've got to get home, but the carousel is all the way back at Celebration Shore," she said. "It will take us *hours* to walk that far. Plus, it's so dark now!"

"What carousel?" Lacey asked.

Amirah turned to look at her. Instantly, her whole face brightened. "Last January, we took a carousel to get home," she said. "How did you and Ziggy get home?"

"By swing!" Lacey replied. "Come on, there's a big park in the middle of Sparkle City . . ." Then she paused. "Except I'm not exactly sure where we are . . ."

Cara shook her head confidently. Her golden horn gleamed in the silvery moonlight. As she trotted down the street, the B-Buds hurried to follow her.

Cara led them straight into the heart of Sparkle City, where a beautiful, emerald-green park stretched out as far as they could see. Just beyond the entrance, Amirah could see a swing set with six swings.

A pink swing. A yellow swing. An orange swing. A green swing. A blue swing. And a purple one.

The colors corresponded perfectly to the carousel that Amirah and her B-Buds had used to travel home last January—*and* to the B-Buds' favorite colors!

"Wait," Olivia said. "Is this goodbye? Until next January? What's going to happen next?"

"I don't know," Amirah said. "But I don't think it's goodbye. Just—see you later. Until the power of sprinkles brings us back here."

"In Jamaica, we say 'inna di morrows' instead of goodbye," Lacey spoke up. "Like—see you in the tomorrows."

"In the tomorrows," Amirah repeated thoughtfully. "I like that a lot! Inna di morrows!"

"Inna di morrows," the B-Buds chorused. It was a promise.

"Tell us what to do," Amirah said to Lacey and Ziggy.

"It's easy!" Lacey said as she hopped onto the orange-colored swing. "Just swing as high and as fast as you can!"

The other B-Buds found their swings too. Then they started to pump their legs.

"Higher!" Lacey encouraged them.

"And faster!" added Ziggy.

As Amirah pumped her legs, her swing zoomed back and forth. Soon she was swinging higher and faster than ever before. The wind whipped her hair as she went up, up, up—

Oh wow, she thought suddenly. *I'm going to go over the top!*

Whoooooosh!

Amirah squeezed her hands tighter on the chains as, sure enough, her swing soared over the top of the swing set—not just once, but again and again. The stars above Sparkle City began to change colors, turning pink and green and blue and purple. They stretched and swirled until they looked like so many sprinkles tumbling through the night sky.

Amirah, dizzy, closed her eyes and waited for the spinning to stop.

CHAPTER NINE

AMIRAH AWOKE WITH A START. It was so dark that she wasn't sure, at first, where she was. Then she spotted her rainbow nightlight glowing on the wall and realized, all in a rush, that she was back home, safe in her room, safe in her bed.

And completely wide-awake!

All of Amirah's memories from her visit to the Magical Land of Birthdays came rushing back. She scrambled out of bed and turned on the light. There were two things she needed: her birthday book and *The Power of Sprinkles*. Intuition told her she was getting close to finding out the identity of the Birthday Basher, and she knew that there was no time to lose.

Amirah opened her birthday book and frantically flipped the pages to July 8. Sure enough, there was the name she expected to see: BILLY BONILLA.

Her own neighbor.

"What happened, Billy?" Amirah whispered sadly. "Why do you hate birthdays so much?"

Amirah was beyond curious, but she knew the reason didn't matter as much as the solution. She opened *The Power of Sprinkles* and scanned each page, searching for Billy's name.

Just then, Amirah realized that she hadn't seen Billy's name in the book before. What if he didn't have a special birthday cake anymore? His cake in the Hall of Birthday Cakes was so rotten that she couldn't even tell what kind it was.

Amirah shook her head as she continued to page through the book. *The Power of Sprinkles* had never let her down before.

Just then, the page beneath her fingertips started to glow with a warm golden light. Tiny sparks traveled from the page onto her fingers, then up her hand, past her wrist, over her arm . . .

Amirah's heart leaped. She remembered when this had happened before and her very own special birthday cake had been revealed. Was another special cake about to be unveiled?

The words appeared as if by magic—birthday magic.

BILLY'S BIRTHDAY CAKE: THIS GOLDEN CARROT CAKE IS FIT FOR ROYALTY!

Fit for royalty? Amirah thought in surprise. The Birthday Basher had once been the Prince of the Magical Land of Birthdays. This seemed like another sign that she was on the right track.

Wistfully, Amirah glanced toward her bedroom door. She wished she could go down to the kitchen right now and start baking Billy's special birthday cake. But Mama and Baba would probably hear her banging around the kitchen, and they would *not* be happy to find her baking in the middle of the night. No, it would just have to wait until morning.

As Amirah climbed into bed, a new thought struck her. *There could be dozens of people named Billy Bonilla in the world. Hundreds! And surely some of them share the same birthday. Maybe even July 8.*

As Amirah rested her head against her smiley-face pillow, she remembered that Billy had named his dog Fiesta. Didn't that suggest that he loved birthdays and parties?

The Birthday Basher used to love birthdays too, she reminded herself.

Amirah's eyes started to close from sheer exhaustion. She knew it didn't really matter if her neighbor Billy was the Birthday Basher or not. His birthday was just a couple days away.

And who wouldn't love to be surprised by a special birthday cake?

AMIRAH AWOKE WITH the first light, filled with energy and purpose. She jumped out of bed, put on her pink baking overalls, and went straight to the kitchen—only to realize that she was up so early that even her parents weren't awake yet.

Amirah knew that she wasn't supposed to use the oven without an adult nearby, but she could still prepare all the ingredients for the cake. Sugar and cinnamon, flour and vanilla. And of course—carrots!

"You're up early." Mama's voice carried into the kitchen from the doorway.

Amirah looked up and grinned. "Good morning!" she called out. "It's Billy's birthday tomorrow, so I thought I'd make him a cake."

"Billy . . . ?" Mama said, looking confused.

"You know, the boy who lives around the corner? He's always walking all the dogs?" Amirah reminded her.

"Oh yes, of course," Mama replied. If Mama was surprised that Amirah was baking a cake for someone she barely knew, she didn't show it. "Do you need any help?"

Amirah looked at the recipe and the neat line of ingredients she had set upon the counter. Then she listened to her heart.

"I got this," she said confidently. "But I'll call you if I get stuck."

"Sounds like a good plan," Mama said with a smile.

Then Amirah went to work! She grated carrots and whisked eggs. She measured sugar and vanilla. She sifted flour and cinnamon. Then she poured the batter, the color of an orange sunrise and flecked with specks of fragrant cinnamon, into the sheet pan—and popped it into the oven.

Mama never needed to use a timer to know when a cake was perfectly done, but the Birthday Basher had been so disappointed in his birthday before that Amirah didn't want to take any chances. Not only did she set the timer, but she refused to leave the kitchen until the cake was done. Soon the whole house smelled like the sweet spices of carrot cake.

While the cake cooled on the countertop, Amirah mixed up the frosting. This cake called for a special step after it was cooled and frosted: It would be painted gold to make it gleam like the real precious metal! Amirah couldn't wait to see what the finished cake would look like.

After Amirah finished frosting Billy's cake, she carefully painted the whole top and sides gold. She stood back to admire it. *It really is fit for royalty*, Amirah thought, remembering how the cake was described in *The Power of Sprinkles*.

If Billy truly was the prince of the Magical Land of Birthdays—at least, before he

became the Birthday Basher—would this special cake be enough to restore his birthday magic?

At this point, Amirah could only wait and see—and hope.

Billy's birthday was tomorrow, so Amirah slid the cake into the fridge to keep it fresh for him. It smelled so good that she couldn't help wondering how it tasted. She tried to imagine it: the richly spiced, delicately sweetened cake . . . the smooth and creamy frosting . . .

Amirah had never tasted gold cake frosting before, though.

Then Amirah noticed a little smattering of crumbs on the counter and a smear of frosting in the mixing bowl. It wasn't much. But it would be enough for a taste.

Amirah swiped her finger through the frosting, then dabbed it onto the crumbs. When she tasted it, a grin spread across her face. It was even more delicious than she had imagined! *I think Billy will—*

Amirah didn't have a chance to finish her thought. The creamy frosting had barely dissolved in her mouth before all the colors around her began to swirl like a kaleidoscope— the walls of the kitchen started to fade away— the floor fell from beneath her feet—

Anticipation surged through Amirah as she shut her eyes. Just like when she'd made her own special cake from *The Power of Sprinkles,* a single taste was enough to transport her back to the Magical Land of Birthdays. She knew that was where she would be as soon as the world stopped spinning.

What she didn't know, though, was what would happen next.

CHAPTER TEN

WHEN AMIRAH OPENED her eyes, she was back in the Magical Land of Birthdays—but something seemed off. She tried to figure out what it was. The world seemed brighter and more enchanted than she'd ever seen it before. But something was still wrong.

Amirah reached out to grab a shiny pink balloon as it drifted by, but she recoiled when she saw her hand. The edges were fuzzy, almost like a picture out of focus. She stared at her feet, her legs, and her arms and realized that the fuzziness—or whatever it was—had overtaken her entirely.

It's not the Magical Land of Birthdays that's changed, she realized. *It's me.*

Amirah may have looked fuzzy and out of focus, but her mind felt clearer than ever. A strong sense of urgency pushed her forward. She could hear the sounds of a party—snippets of music, loud laughter, the clinking of forks on cake plates—and decided to follow the sounds.

133

Maybe her B-Buds were nearby. Maybe they could help her figure out what was going on.

Amirah walked a short distance until she reached a clearing, where she found a birthday party underway. The table was crowded with B-Buds, she realized—but not *her* B-Buds. This was a different group of friends, bonded by a different shared birthday.

"Hi," Amirah said with a little wave. She hoped that they wouldn't think she was intruding on their celebration.

No one responded. They didn't even look her way.

"Hello!" Amirah tried again.

Still nothing.

Amirah, feeling bolder than ever, walked straight over to the table and squeezed in between two chairs. "Can I have a piece of cake?" she asked.

Still no one responded. And this time, when Amirah tried to lift a cake plate from the table, she realized that her hands weren't able to grasp it.

I'm not really here, she suddenly thought. *They can't see me or hear me. But I can see—and hear—them.*

But Amirah wasn't scared. Something was going to happen; she could just tell. And the Magical Land of Birthdays wanted her to see it.

There were seven kids at the table. There were eleven candles on the cake. *Eleven*, Amirah thought. That was the same age she and her B-Buds were when they had discovered the Magical Land of Birthdays last January.

Amirah began to study the kids at the party. Three girls, four boys—at first she didn't recognize any of them. There was a boy sitting at the far end of the table who was partially turned away from her. There was something familiar about him, though all she could see was his brown hair and the side of his neck.

Then he turned his head as he laughed, and Amirah recognized him at once.

It was Billy.

Her mind whirled as she tried to put everything together, remembering all the details from the story of the Birthday Basher. Billy seemed way too joyful to be single-handedly stripping the happiness from the Magical Land of Birthdays. What could have possibly happened to change him so drastically?

Be patient, Amirah told herself. She had a feeling that before long, all would be revealed.

As soon as the partygoers finished eating birthday cake, their plates disappeared like magic and a present appeared where each plate had been. The B-Buds gasped in delight. Amirah smiled to herself, knowing in her heart that those presents had come from the special tent filled with gifts she had discovered and that each friend was about to open their very own perfect present.

She watched as the B-Buds opened their gifts. A pair of ballet shoes . . . a soccer ball . . . a paint set . . .

And then it was Billy's turn.

He lifted the lid off his present and leaned over to look inside. Whatever was in the box cast a golden light across his face, which seemed to glow with wonderment. Then Billy reached into the box and lifted up a golden crown. Each point was tipped with a glittering gem in a different color of the rainbow.

Or, Amirah thought, beaming, *the color of sprinkles.*

The B-Buds gasped when they saw Billy's gift. "Look! There's a tag!" a girl cried. "What does it say?"

"Read it!" one of the boys added.

Billy lifted up the tag and read. "For the prince of the Magical Land of Birthdays," he said.

Silence fell upon the party.

A sheepish, almost embarrassed smile

crossed Billy's face. "This can't be right," he said. "There must be some mistake. I'm not a prince. I'm just—me."

"Maybe in the regular world," the girl said. "But here—you've always had more birthday magic than anyone else."

"Alicia!" Billy said in surprise.

"It's true, though," Alicia insisted. "You discovered how to get here a whole year before the rest of us. And when we arrived, you found each one of us. You explained what was happening. You showed us how to love birthdays even more than we already did."

"You know she's right," another girl chimed in.

Billy's smile grew more confident. "Birthdays really are the best," he said.

"All hail Prince Billy," one of the boys announced.

Amirah suspected he was just kidding, but

in the somber quiet of the clearing, his words rang too true to be a joke.

Alicia stepped forward and, without a word, took the crown from Billy. She placed it carefully on his head, making sure his crown was straight. "All hail Prince Billy," she repeated.

Billy sat very still for a moment, as if he needed to get used to the weight of the crown on his head. Then he lifted his glass of lemonade for a toast. "To the happiest birthdays, and the best B-Buds ever," he announced. "Cheers!"

"Cheers!" the B-Buds chorused.

Then they began to sing the happy birthday song. Amirah joined in, even though she knew they couldn't hear her. It was her favorite song, after all.

Before the song was half over, though, the world started spinning, and the colors around her started twirling and twisting into new shapes and patterns. She closed her eyes and waited for

the spinning to stop, knowing she'd be home, safe and sound in her very own house once more.

Except that's not what happened. Not this time.

When Amirah opened her eyes again, she was seated on a velvet throne in a dark, windowless room. A screen on the wall across from her flickered to life. She leaned forward, eager to see what would be revealed.

There was a figure on the screen: Billy. He wasn't in the Magical Land of Birthdays, though. Amirah had a feeling that she was watching him back in the real world.

A crown—Billy's crown—glinted on a shelf above his bed. And on his bed, a small brown dog was all curled up.

"It's going to be so great, Fiesta," Billy said from his desk, which was cluttered with art supplies and stacks of red paper.

There were striped treat bags too, which looked vaguely familiar to Amirah, though she couldn't quite place them. Even the invitations Billy was making looked a little familiar, but Amirah was certain she'd never seen them before.

She turned her attention back to Billy, who was busy writing something on a red piece of paper. "The best birthday party ever, right here in my own house, with my B-Buds from all around the world!" he was saying.

Fiesta's tail went *thump-thump-thump*.

"Birthday magic can bring them here, I know it," Billy said. "I *feel* it."

Amirah sat up a little straighter. She knew exactly the feeling he meant.

"It won't matter that they live all over the world when they get their invitations," Billy confided in his dog. "My birthday magic is strong enough to bring them here. It's strong enough to do anything!"

Billy sat back and looked at the six invitations on his desk. He placed a handmade friendship bracelet on each one. Then a grin flashed across his face. "Almost forgot something!" he said as he reached for a jar of sprinkles. He added a smattering of sprinkles to each card as he tucked them into envelopes. "Like confetti, but better. Right, Fiesta?"

Amirah smiled to herself as Billy popped a handful of sprinkles in his mouth before he sealed the envelopes. They had so much more in common than she would've thought. At least, they did—before he became the Birthday Basher.

She watched the screen as Billy took his invitations outside and put them in the mailbox on the corner. "See you soon, B-Buds," he whispered.

Then he went home, whistling the birthday song.

Amirah sat up a little straighter as the mailbox on the corner started to tremble. The sky got brighter and brighter. Then, in a flash of blinding light, all six invitations soared out of the mailbox!

Wow, she thought in astonishment. *Billy figured out how to use birthday magic in the real world! How did he do it?*

But as Amirah watched, the invitations didn't split up to travel to Billy's B-Buds around the globe. Instead, they flew, almost in formation, up into the sky, past the clouds, past the sun, until all the stars of deep space swirled into a kaleidoscope of colors . . .

When the film came into focus again, Amirah realized that the special invitations hadn't been delivered to Billy's B-Buds after all.

"The sprinkles," Amirah whispered to herself. Somehow Billy had made a terrible mistake. The sprinkles he'd added to the envelopes hadn't helped his invitations get to his B-Buds.

They'd transported the invitations to the Magical Land of Birthdays instead!

Amirah watched in horror as the invitations sat, untouched, on a rock. Then a breeze kicked up, blowing them onto the dirt. One of the invitations got stuck in the crook of a tree. The wind grew stronger and stronger until it tore part of the envelope, which fluttered away like a speck of confetti.

Amirah gasped. She suddenly realized why the invitations had looked familiar: It wasn't litter or confetti that Amirah and her B-Buds had been gathering all over the Magical Land of Birthdays.

It was the shredded remains of Billy's lost invitations!

Before Amirah could fully grasp the seriousness of the situation, the image on the screen dissolved, and a new image appeared: a beautiful room that was all decorated for a party, with a long table that was filled with party favors, cookies, and a gorgeous sheet cake with gold frosting.

"Where is everybody?" Amirah asked. From what she could see, there was only one guest at this party: Billy, who was wearing his birthday crown.

He turned around in his chair, and that's when Amirah saw his face. It was twisted into a terrible grimace of disappointment, rage, and despair. Billy's joyful smile was gone, and his eyes looked small and mean. He sat completely still, staring at the empty chairs all around him.

Without warning, Billy stood up. He lifted the entire cake—candles and all—and threw the whole thing into the trash with one fast movement.

Amirah gasped in shock.

But what happened next was even worse.

"Stupid birthdays," Billy muttered to himself. "Worthless, pointless, *stupid* birthdays!"

Then he took off his crown—his perfect present—and threw it at the wall so hard that it cracked.

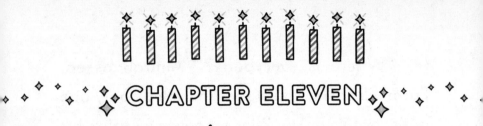

CHAPTER ELEVEN

THERE WAS A SUDDEN *WHOOSH*, and Amirah found herself jerked from the velvet throne into a dark, windy tunnel. She might have been afraid, but she still had faith in birthday magic—and especially the power of sprinkles. As her fingers curled around the vial of sprinkles in her pocket, she saw the familiar bright streaks of colorful light. Her shoulders relaxed as she sighed with relief. Amirah knew where she was going now.

Home.

She found herself back in the kitchen, holding on to the counter to steady herself as she tried to make sense of everything she'd seen. So that was how the prince of the Magical Land of Birthdays had lost his birthday magic and turned into the Birthday Basher. It had seemed like such an impossible transformation before, but now that she'd seen Billy's heartbreak, Amirah could understand . . . sort of. She thought of her own birthday parties with a pang of sorrow. Amirah loved a big party—the bigger the better! She invited everyone in her town, from the mayor to the principal of her school. She tried to imagine what it would feel like if no one showed up.

She'd be devastated.

I wonder if Billy even knows that he's the Birthday Basher, Amirah thought. *If he has any idea of what is happening in the Magical Land of Birthdays. What if his birthday magic is so powerful that when it turned into a force for darkness, it became unstoppable?*

Then she stopped.

The trouble wasn't just in the Magical Land of Birthdays.

It was in her very own neighborhood.

On her street.

Perhaps, even, in her mailbox.

Billy's party invitations never arrived where they needed to go, Amirah thought slowly.

Neither did some of Paulina's invitations. And Mom mentioned Amir missing a party because of a lost invitation.

Everything was starting to make sense, in the worst way. Billy was the neighborhood dog walker. He took long walks in the neighborhood twice a day. He had plenty of opportunities to peek into his neighbors' mailboxes. And if he spotted a colorful birthday party invitation . . .

And took it . . .

And—what did he do next? Throw it away? Tear it to shreds?

Amirah didn't really want to know.

With a sigh, she stood up and walked over to the fridge. She opened the door and stared at Billy's special birthday cake. The golden frosting gleamed in the light of the fridge. A small, sad smile crossed Amirah's face as she remembered the kind of cake Billy had tossed in the trash at his lonely birthday party.

It was a carrot cake, of course. His favorite.

Will a special birthday cake be enough to fix everything? Amirah wondered.

She shook her head, as if to shake away all her doubts. *You just have to believe*, Amirah reminded herself.

Then a new idea struck her. What if she left Billy's cake in his mailbox? He'd been taking things from other people's mailboxes. Maybe finding a special surprise in his own mailbox would help make things right.

Amirah pulled Billy's cake out of the fridge and studied it. The flat sheet cake was way too big to fit in a mailbox. But Amirah knew how to fix that.

First, she whipped up a new batch of frosting. Then she sliced the cake into two equal halves and used the extra frosting to stack one half on top of the other. Making steady, careful cuts, Amirah trimmed the edges of the cake. Now, instead of a large, flat rectangle, it had more height. Using the gold paint, Amirah touched up the edges and sides of the cake. When she was finished, it looked like a solid-gold bar. It was truly fit for a prince.

Amirah tucked Billy's cake back in the fridge, then put the cake scraps on a plate and saved them for later. She had a feeling that this cake was too important to go to waste.

Billy's special birthday cake was ready at last. But there was one more thing that Amirah wanted to do. She hurried over to the closet where Mama kept all her sewing supplies and rummaged around until she found just what she needed: yarn in seven bright rainbow colors. Then Amirah carried the yarn up to her bedroom. There wasn't a lot of time, but if she worked hard, she knew she could make seven rainbow-colored friendship bracelets in time for tomorrow.

◇ ✧ ◇

THE NEXT MORNING, Amirah woke with the first light. The big day was finally here—Billy's birthday. This was Amirah's chance to restore his faith in birthdays. To turn his birthday magic back into a force for good. And—hopefully—to save the Magical Land of Birthdays too.

She got dressed quickly and made sure to put the friendship bracelets and her vial of sprinkles into her pockets. Then Amirah slipped downstairs, took Billy's cake out of the fridge, and stepped outside.

The sunrise made the golden frosting gleam brighter than ever. She walked quickly and quietly to Billy's house, then put the cake in his mailbox and ran all the way home.

Back inside, Amirah pressed her hand over her pounding heart and tried to catch her breath. That's when she suddenly realized something: It wasn't just Billy's birthday. It was also her half birthday! She remembered the scraps of Billy's cake that were still in the fridge and smiled to herself. Maybe eating a little cake on her half birthday could become a new tradition!

As she served herself a plate of cake, Amirah couldn't help thinking of her B-Buds all over the world. She had a feeling that they would remember it was their half birthday too. She wished she could see them. It didn't feel right to celebrate even a half birthday without her B-Buds nearby.

Just before she took a bite of cake, Amirah had an idea. She took the sprinkles out of her pocket and carefully selected one in each color: pink, orange, yellow, green, blue, purple. Then—because it was their half birthdays after all—she broke each one in half and placed half of each sprinkle on her cake.

Amirah took a big bite and grinned. This bite of Billy's cake was even more delicious than the taste she'd had in her kitchen.

But before she could take another bite—

Whoosh!

CHAPTER TWELVE

BACK AGAIN, **AMIRAH THOUGHT** with a smile as she arrived, once more, in the Magical Land of Birthdays. It was early morning here too; pale pink light from the sunrise was spilling into the sky. Pink. Her favorite color. That seemed just right.

Amirah stood up, brushed the dust off her clothes, and looked around. It was still too dark to see very far, but she had a feeling she wasn't alone. "B-Buds?" she called. "Is anyone here?"

There was a rustling in the darkness.

"I'm here," said a voice.

"Me too," said another.

"And me."

"B-Buds!"

There was a sudden burst of light from Ziggy's watch—just enough for Amirah and her B-Buds to see one another. They all rushed forward at the same time and collided in a big hug. Everyone started talking at once until Lacey's voice carried above the chatter.

"Hey—*hey!*" she announced. "Let Amirah speak! I want to know what she learned about the Birthday Basher!"

As the other B-Buds grew quiet, Lacey turned to Amirah. "Did you find him?" she asked. "Is it your neighbor?"

So much had happened in the short time since she'd seen her B-Buds that Amirah hardly knew where to begin. The words tumbled out in a big rush as she told them everything she could remember—especially the part about how Billy transformed from the prince of the Magical Land of Birthdays to the Birthday Basher.

There was another silence when Amirah finally finished.

"So—what now?" Elvis asked with a note of hesitation in his voice.

"I left the cake in his mailbox," Amirah explained. "Hopefully, when he takes a bite, it will bring him here—"

"Here?" Olivia repeated, her voice like a squeak. "He can't come back here! He's already done enough to ruin the Magical Land of Birthdays!"

"Don't you understand?" Amirah asked, holding her palms up. "The Unha—I mean Billy—*has* to come back here. I can't think of a better place to restore his birthday magic to the way it used to be."

"We have bigger problems than Billy right now," Mei said, pointing at the sky. "Look at those clouds!"

All the B-Buds turned to look. Amirah had seen lots of different weather changes in the Magical Land of Birthdays, but these gathering clouds were unusually ominous. They looked dangerous, almost. The sky billowed with them, dark purple like smashed blackberries, as they swirled above—

"That's the Rainbow Forest," Amirah said thoughtfully. She glanced sideways at

Olivia, remembering how the B-Buds had found Olivia hiding in the Rainbow Forest when she was struggling with her own birthday disappointment last winter.

Could Billy be there too?

Were the clouds a manifestation of how his birthday magic had changed?

Was their darkness drawn to him?

There was only one way to find out.

"Come on," Amirah said as she started walking toward the Rainbow Forest. "Let's find Billy."

No one else moved.

"Hold on," Mei said. "I think we should leave. I've never seen a sky like that before. It's not safe here."

"If Billy ate his cake and returned to the Magical Land of Birthdays, why is it still so dark and dreary?" Ziggy pointed out. "And it's only getting worse. What if he's come back to destroy the land—forever?"

Olivia shivered and rubbed her arms. "I don't want to come back here again," she said, glancing around anxiously. "It's not the way it used to be. I don't think it can be fixed."

"B-Buds," Amirah said urgently. "Listen to me. We didn't come back just to give up!"

She rummaged around in her pocket, then pulled out the friendship bracelets she'd made. "I made one of these for each of you," she said as she passed them out. "So that we can always be connected, even when we're far apart.

"Here's the thing, though—we're *not* far apart right now," Amirah continued. "We're together, and that doesn't happen nearly enough. We've all come to the Magical Land of Birthdays, not on our birthday but on our half birthday. I think that's important. I think it matters. I think we need to find Billy—*together.*"

Lacey twisted her new friendship bracelet around her wrist. "But, Amirah—how do you *know* it's safe?" she asked.

"I don't," Amirah said simply. "Sometimes, you just have to believe. And I'll never stop believing in birthday magic, never, no matter what. If we don't at least *try* to fix things, we'll be giving up on birthday magic—just like Billy.

"So . . . who's with me?" she finished.

There was a pause.

Then Elvis clapped his hand on Amirah's arm. "I am," he said.

"Me too," added Lacey.

Ziggy stepped forward. "And me."

Finally, Mei and Olivia spoke at the same time. "Me too."

Amirah felt a surge of gratitude in her heart. "Let's do this," she said. "B-Buds together— forever!"

The six friends set off for the Rainbow Forest. Overhead, the clouds grew thicker and more threatening. Thunder rumbled so close that it made the ground tremble. Not far away, the edge of the Rainbow Forest waited. The colors were completely washed out. All Amirah could see were different shades of gray.

The B-Buds were silent as they stepped into the woods with Amirah in the lead. Deeper and deeper into the forest they traveled until Amirah stopped suddenly.

Just ahead, there was a clearing that glowed with otherworldly light. It was hard to see the gathering storm that was brewing through the thick trees, but if Amirah had to guess, she would say they were right under the heart of it.

"There," she whispered to the B-Buds. "I think Billy's in there. Come on."

Amirah took a few steps before she realized she was walking alone. She turned around to her B-Buds in surprise.

"Aren't you—" she began.

Elvis's smile was a little crooked. "We'll be right here," he promised, "if you need us. But I don't think you will."

"But—" Amirah said.

"It's you. Don't you know that? It was always you." Mei spoke up. "You're the one from the book—the one with enough birthday magic to stop the Birthday Basher. You're the one with the power to fix this."

Amirah nodded slowly. In her heart, she hoped they were right.

Then she reminded herself one more time: *Believe.*

She took a few more steps into the clearing. As she got closer, she saw a lone figure sitting in the middle of the strange light. The light was shifting, changing. She realized that there wasn't just one source for it but hundreds— maybe even thousands. It was one of the most enchanting sights she'd ever seen.

"Billy?" she asked.

The figure turned around.

It was him—the Birthday Basher.

It was Billy!

A shy smile crossed his face.

"Hi, Amirah," he said. "Thanks for the cake. It was delicious. Carrot cake is my favorite. And that gold bar shape—it was truly special."

"I'm so glad you liked it," she replied, smiling back. "Happy birthday!"

Billy took a deep breath. "I thought I'd lost it," he said. "My birthday magic. I thought it was gone forever. But look—look at this!"

Amirah stepped closer and realized that Billy was holding something in his hands: a ball of light. No, it wasn't a ball of light, but a ball of rainbow sprinkles that shifted and danced on an unseen current, casting a rainbow glow that spread throughout the whole clearing.

"Wow," she breathed. "That's incredible!"

"I didn't think it would ever come back," he said.

"All you have to do is believe," she told him.

Billy's smile faded a little bit. "Sometimes that's not so easy to do," he replied.

Amirah sat down across from him. "Listen,

Billy," she began. "I have to tell you something. Your B-Buds didn't skip your party on purpose."

Billy didn't say anything as he stared at the ground.

"They never even got the invitations," Amirah continued.

Billy looked up, a startled expression on his face.

"Somehow they came to the Magical Land of Birthdays instead," Amirah explained. She held out a handful of the faded red confetti that she and her B-Buds had been gathering throughout the land.

"My invitations were bright red," Billy said slowly.

"Yes, they were," Amirah replied. "A year ago. But since then, they've been fluttering around the Magical Land of Birthdays, exposed to rain and sun and wind."

"The paper faded," Billy realized.

"Yes," Amirah said again. "I have something else for you too."

She gave him the last friendship bracelet from her pocket.

"I know you have your own B-Buds," she said. "But I was thinking—since we're neighbors and we share half birthdays—maybe you could be one of my honorary B-Buds. I made these bracelets for all of us."

She gestured back toward the edge of the clearing, where the other B-Buds waved.

"An honorary B-Bud," Billy said, trying out the words. "I guess that means we could celebrate birthdays every six months."

"The more celebrating, the better!" Amirah declared.

This time, when Billy smiled, it was bigger and brighter than ever. He slipped the bracelet onto his wrist—

The swirling ball of glowing sprinkles that

Billy had been holding suddenly exploded, scattering sparks of light and color throughout the Rainbow Forest—and all over the Magical Land of Birthdays!

The B-Buds rushed into the clearing, shrieking and cheering in celebration. They were making so much noise that at first none of them could hear the clattering of hoofbeats across the ground.

Amirah could feel them, though. She turned away from the group just in time to see Cara the Unicorn enter with a gift box balanced on her back.

"Another present?" Amirah exclaimed. She turned to Billy. "You'd better open it. It's your birthday, after all."

"Okay," Billy replied. Everyone crowded around to watch him open the present—and gasped when they realized what was inside: a golden crown!

The same one, Amirah realized, that

Billy had thrown at the wall. She recognized the crack. As he lifted it out of the box, the crack disappeared like magic. Birthday magic.

"It's like new!" Billy said in surprise. "Almost new. It's just missing some jewels . . ."

Amirah tilted her head to the side as she studied the hollow places in the crown. Suddenly, she had an idea. She picked up one of the dull red scraps left from Billy's invitations and pressed it against the crown. There was a *pop* of sparks, and when the smoke cleared, a red gem sparkled in its place.

Amirah grinned at Billy and the other B-Buds. "Looks like we can fix that!" she said.

All the B-Buds helped create new jewels on the crown, until it really was good as new.

Amirah held the crown in both hands and presented it to Billy. "For the prince of the Magical Land of Birthdays," she announced.

Billy took the crown from her and looked at it for a long moment. Then, to everyone's surprise, he reached out and placed it ever so gently on Amirah's head. "For the *princess*," he corrected her. "I think this crown belongs to you now."

"But—" Amirah began.

"I mean it," Billy said. "I have to get used to having my birthday magic back, anyway. Besides—you deserve it."

"Billy! Hey, Billy!"

Everyone turned to look at the edge of the clearing. There were six kids standing there, three girls and three boys. Amirah recognized them right away.

They were Billy's B-Buds!

"We've been looking everywhere for you!" one of the girls called out. "Come on! It's time to celebrate our birthday!"

Slowly, a grin spread across Billy's face. "My B-Buds," he said. "They're here!"

"Have the best birthday ever, Billy," Amirah said, beaming. "See you back in the neighborhood!"

"See you!" Billy replied. Then he ran off to join his B-Buds. Their happy chatter echoed through the Rainbow Forest as they set off for a birthday celebration.

"I guess it's up to us to crown the princess," Mei said.

"I just don't know . . ." Amirah replied.

Olivia smiled. "*You* might not know—but we do," she replied. "You're the one, Amirah! The one from the book. The one with enough birthday magic to stop the Birthday Basher and bring back joy to the Magical Land of Birthdays."

And without another word, Amirah's B-Buds took hold of the crown and placed it on her head.

It wasn't too heavy. In fact, it felt just right. She looked at each one of her B-Buds, all of them smiling encouragingly. They'd been through so much over the past few days. Amirah knew it would take some time for her to process everything that had happened. But that could wait. Right now, they were together—on their half birthday—which could only mean one thing:

It was time to celebrate!

ABOUT THE AUTHOR

FLOUR SHOP founder and Flour-ist Amirah Kassem is an artist at heart and cake is her medium. Amirah is the bestselling author of *The Power of Sprinkles*. Amirah grew up baking and sculpting with her mother in Mexico, where she discovered an appreciation for fine ingredients—and mastered the art of multisensory experiences.